DEAD END

Dead End, Arizona, was just another whistle-stop on the way to nowhere. But in Dead End the future of humanity depended upon the actions of a few brave souls . . . and an army of supernatural creatures with no souls at all! Earth could be invaded by another planet if they lost the war — but if they won, the battle between the living and the undead would continue . . . Either way, the streets of Dead End were going to run with blood.

STEVE HAYES
AND
DAVID WHITEHEAD

DEAD END

Complete and Unabridged

LINFORD
Leicester

First published in Great Britain

First Linford Edition
published 2010

British Library CIP Data

Whitehead, David, *1958* –
  Dead end. - - (Linford mystery library)
  1. Horror tales.
  2. Large type books.
  I. Title II. Series
  823.9′14–dc22

  ISBN 978–1–44480–188–0

Published by
F. A. Thorpe (Publishing)
Anstey, Leicestershire

Set by Words & Graphics Ltd.
Anstey, Leicestershire
Printed and bound in Great Britain by
T. J. International Ltd., Padstow, Cornwall

This book is printed on acid-free paper

1

They say that a man's spirit drops to its lowest point sometime around three in the morning, and that was certainly the case with Officer Ruben Rivera of the Arizona State Department of Public Safety.

Five tedious hours into a so-far routine eight-hour shift, Rivera was just stifling yet another jaw-cracking yawn when he spotted a battered Ford Ranger up ahead, parked slantwise across the shoulder of the isolated desert road.

A stocky, olive-skinned man in his early thirties, the state trooper immediately slowed to a cautious twenty, then wheeled over and parked his SUV yards behind it.

Doing his best to shake off his fatigue (for the noisy comings and goings of the extended Rivera family made it impossible to sleep for any length of time during the day), he took his Maglite from the glove compartment, snatched up his flat-brimmed, pinch-crowned hat, and climbed out.

The night was cold and lonely. Silver-grey clouds scuttled across the full moon like Rorschach inkblots. Moonlight, headlights and flashlight were all that held the otherwise near-total darkness at bay.

Suppressing a shiver, Rivera played his beam over the truck. It was about six or seven years old, pale blue and poorly-maintained. Both the engine and headlights had been switched off. It appeared to have been abandoned.

Next he gave his surroundings a quick, searching glance. In the blink and flicker of the SUV's rotating red and blue roof-lights, the tall saguaros with which the wilderness was studded looked like green stick-men trying to touch heaven.

He moved a little closer. Somewhere out in the night, a wolf howled.

Rivera stopped and listened, puzzled by the mournful howl. Mexican red wolves seldom crossed the border into Arizona and the fact that this one had was worth taking note of. The howl came again. He grimaced. God, he hated that sound, always had. Although he was a second generation American, he was still a Mexican at heart, and as everyone knew, Mexicans were a superstitious people and he was no exception.

In this day and age, of course, it was crazy to give credence to such childish beliefs: that if you dropped a tortilla on the floor, you were going to have visitors; that if you put your shoes on the bed, someone close to you was going to die; that a pregnant woman should never touch her belly during an eclipse.

These ridiculous maxims, the so-called power of the *mal ojo* and more; Rivera didn't believe in them exactly, but having been raised mostly by superstitious grandparents, neither was he in any special hurry to dismiss them. He was a cautious man, and as such had no particular desire to tempt fate.

As he approached the truck, he saw that the driver's-side door had been left open. He was just about to take a look inside when he glimpsed a fluid dash of movement in the darkness away to his right.

He quickly shone his light in that

direction, but illuminated only big, amber rocks and breeze-ruffled brush.

Somewhere close by, the wolf howled a third time.

Unsnapping the safety-strap that held his Sig Sauer P226 in its holster, he returned his attention to the truck. The hood was still warm to the touch, so it hadn't been parked here long. He shone the light across the ground, searching for tracks. There were no signs of violence that he could see.

Finally he pointed the flashlight into the cab. The keys were still in the ignition, and some books were scattered across the passenger seat.

He played the light over them. They looked old and well-thumbed, and had titles like *Ancient Legends and Curses, Self-Hypnosis* and *Demons Within Us*.

Rivera frowned.

He reached inside and was about to pull the nearest book closer when, above the whine of the strengthening wind, he heard a soft crackle of sound behind him. He spun, pulling his gun free at the same moment.

The misty bar of torchlight swept around in a short, fast arc, pinpointing a dark shape just beyond a stand of spiky graythorn twenty feet away. The figure immediately froze and raised his slender, long-fingered hands.

'Whoa! Hold on. Don't shoot!'

Rivera released a trapped breath. 'All right,' he said, still keeping the newcomer covered. 'Come closer and keep your hands where I can see 'em.'

The figure obeyed, making more brittle crackling sounds as he stepped carefully through an assault course of cholla, saltbush and scattered rocks.

The flashlight showed Rivera an athletic-looking stubble-jawed man of around average height. Late twenties or early thirties, he had a narrow, moderately handsome face that was now squinting in the harsh torchlight. He had hazel eyes, a short straight nose and a wide mouth, and his curly light brown hair fell in an untidy spill across his forehead.

'What're you doing out here?' asked Rivera.

'Taking a leak.'

'Then how come you're all covered in dirt?'

The man glanced down at himself, almost in surprise. His black leather All-Son bomber jacket, green shirt and khaki twill pants were torn in places and powdered with dust.

'I, uh, tripped in the dark,' he said, 'and fell into a bunch of mesquite.'

The state trooper weighed his answer silently. The man looked worn and exhausted. Rivera wondered why. 'What's your name, mister?'

'Ed Knight.'

'Let me see your license and registration.'

Moving carefully, Ed handed the documents over. As he leaned forward to take them, Rivera sniffed. He couldn't smell any booze on the man, nor the tell-tale tang of mints to disguise it. And when he looked Knight in the eye, his pupils appeared normal, not dilated as you'd expect from someone using drugs.

Ed turned his knitted collar up against the wind while the trooper checked his papers. Shortly, Rivera handed the documents back and said, 'Seems okay.

Where you headed, Mr Knight?'

'Dead End.'

'Nice place.'

'So I've heard.'

'Well, best be on your way,' advised the state trooper, stifling another yawn. 'And watch how far you stray next time nature calls. It's easy for a man to get lost out here — and easier still for a careless one to get lost for *good*.'

★ ★ ★

Ed remembered those words again thirty miles later, when he ran smack into a dust-storm.

The wind had been gathering itself for a big blow all night, playing hell with his radio reception. Now, as he finally lost KDKB altogether, it began to swipe at the truck with tremendous force, and he had to fight the wheel to hold it steady.

Moments later he saw the dust directly ahead, and his heart raced fearfully.

Rushing toward him was a solid, mustard-coloured wall, at least a mile high and God knew how long. It reached for him like a bed-sheet flipped out across a lumpy mattress, and he quickly switched the wipers on full.

Seconds later the storm swallowed him whole. He clenched his teeth as it howled around him and did its best to smother the beams of his headlights.

The wind slapped the old pickup hard, causing it to rock precariously and veer from right to left. Sand started to pile up in the well where the wipers usually sat. The radio suddenly blared back to life, and he had just enough time to recognise Aerosmith's *Bone to Bone* before it died again.

He knew if he had any sense he'd pull over and sit it out, but he couldn't afford any more delays. He had places to go and things to do. Besides, the events of the night had left him exhausted and he wasn't thinking as clearly as he might.

The wipers continued to squeak back and forth but made little difference to his visibility, which was now practically zero. Soon they slowed and juddered sluggishly across the smeared windshield. A few moments later they stopped altogether.

Ed swore and hunched over the wheel, trying to see the way ahead more clearly.

Instead, a signpost loomed up in front of him and he grimly realised that he had strayed off the road.

He swore again, stamped on the brake and spun the wheel. But he was too late —

The truck slammed into the post. It broke in half, the top section, bearing the sign itself, crashing down onto the hood and then ramming forward to smash through the windshield. It clipped Ed on the temple and slammed him back in his seat. Warm blood spilled down into his eyes.

Then things went from bad to worse.

Stunned and no longer aware of his actions, he inadvertently jammed his foot down on the gas pedal and sent the truck bouncing across the desert floor with the high-pitched protest of the engine only adding to his disorientation.

The radio came back on. Steven Tyler was singing:

'*Ooh, runnin' with the pack,*
Ooh, and never lookin' back,

*Ooh, and knows just where he's
been . . .* '

Seconds later the truck punched into a
dune and came to an abrupt, bone-jarring
halt. Ed was thrown forward, his sternum
crunching hard against the steering wheel
. . . but by then he'd lost consciousness
altogether and was mercifully beyond
further pain.

Around him, the storm raged on.

2

With its eye-catching silver-white body-work and flush black privacy windows, the Prevost Entertainer tour bus was a magnificent thing to behold.

A distinctive, splinter-edged logo ran the length of both sides. In the brightest fluorescent orange it read *PLATINUM DEAD* — the name of the band who had commissioned it.

Almost fifty feet in length, the bus had been custom-built to the band's very definite specifications. It boasted four separate wood-panelled lounge areas, four separate sleeping areas, two work stations complete with wireless internet terminals, three television areas, a bath/shower room, fully-stocked galley kitchen and dining table.

There was extra head-room, extra leg-room, three spacious under-floor cargo bays, a padded leather ceiling and a state-of-the-art In-Motion Datron satellite system.

11

It had everything.

Everything, that was, except air conditioning.

That was the one thing the band's single roadie, Gerry Irwin, couldn't understand. When he'd first set about familiarising himself with the controls, he'd asked Jake Simms, the lead singer, how they were supposed to switch it on or off.

'We don't,' said Jake.

'What, you mean it works itself?'

'I mean there isn't any.'

'*What?* Are you saying they forgot to install it?'

'No. I'm saying we didn't want it.'

Gerry couldn't believe his ears. 'Aw, *shoot*, man! We're gonna be travelling through Arizona. Arizona in the summertime! It's gonna be like an oven in this damn' thing!'

Fixing him with a flat, black-eyed stare, Jake said quietly, 'That's the way we like it.'

But it wasn't the way Gerry Irwin liked it.

A chunky man in his late thirties, with

an unkempt mop of bleach-streaked mouse-brown hair crowning a round, shaggy-bearded face, he'd always been musically-minded and had worked with musicians practically his entire life, having started out with a local garage band whilst still in high school.

Branded a geek by his peers because of his keen interest in science and technology, the then-sixteen year-old had figured that fetching and carrying for a band would be a good way to meet chicks.

As things had turned out, it wasn't. But he'd picked up plenty of practical experience, and fallen in love with the roadie lifestyle.

From roadie he'd eventually moved up — literally — to steel dog, erecting scaffolding for better bands at bigger gigs. He was good at what he did. Even-tempered and thorough, bands loved him because he was easy to get along with and could always be relied upon to tune and fix drums, bass and keyboards just the way they liked them.

But eventually the hedonistic life that went with the job caught up with him.

And after years of alcohol and amphetamine abuse, he'd suffered a minor heart attack — a wake-up call, his doctors said.

Agreeing with the assessment, Gerry had decided that the time had come to clean up his act. But it hadn't been easy, not even with his system pumped full of Risperidone, Clozapine, Haloperidol and Xanax.

For long, haunted months he'd lurched between hyperactivity and exhaustion, insomnia and over-sleeping. He'd suffered shakes and seizures and languished in the deepest, darkest pits of near-suicidal depression and anxiety.

But as tempting as it had been to do so, not once had he ever considered giving up; because to give up meant to go back to the kind of life he'd led before, which would almost certainly kill him, and he dearly didn't want that.

So he'd squared his shoulders and fought his demons and, surprising no one more than himself, had eventually beaten them all.

There was just one problem.

By the time he was fit enough to go

back to work, no one wanted to hire him. The heart attack had turned him into a liability, they said, and liabilities were one of those pesky little things that insurance companies didn't like.

Near-broke and living alone in a greasy, single-wide trailer just south of Search-light, Nevada, he began to binge-eat. Worse, he also started drinking again.

Until, right out of the blue, the *Platinum Dead* hired him.

Gerry had never heard of them before, but they seemed pretty sure they were heading for the top. And when he finally got to see their factory-new tour bus he told himself that someone else must think so too, to have bankrolled them to such an extent.

Now, forty pounds overweight but just glad to be working again, he did as he was told and didn't make waves or question the band's odd behaviour.

But it *was* odd.

Take this morning, for example.

Without any warning Jake had appeared silently at his shoulder and told him to pull up alongside the straight desert road because they wanted to meditate.

Meditate!

Gerry started to remind him about their schedule, a schedule he, Jack-of-all-trades Gerry, was responsible for maintaining, but one flat glare from Jake shut him up.

Five minutes later the band left the bus and walked off about forty yards into the desert, leaving Gerry to switch on the little Vornado Air Circulator he'd fixed to the dashboard.

Once they'd chosen their spot, Jake, Beau, Brad and Kyle had sketched some patterns in the hot sand. One showed a crescent moon with a four-pointed star between its two curved points. The second showed an upside-down crescent moon with no star, and the third depicted a sun with spike-shaped rays emanating from it.

Their work complete, the four band-members then sat cross-legged in a rough circle around the pictographs, eyes half-closed and lips occasionally twitching.

Gerry took off his sweat-darkened baseball cap and ran the back of one podgy hand across his forehead. He held off as long as he could, but twenty minutes later, with no real choice in the matter if they were to stick to their itinerary, he reluctantly pressed the horn.

The harsh *blat* of sound washed out across the vast, open desert, shattering its hitherto pristine silence. At first the four band-members gave no sign that they had even heard it. But when Jake finally glanced toward the bus, they grudgingly got to their feet.

They slouched back through the brush and rocks, looking no different than a hundred similar acts Gerry had worked with over the years.

As one they wore their long, multi-coloured hair cut in staggered layers. Jake's was black, shot through with single streaks of white and blue. Beau's had green and orange high-lights, Brad's black and yellow, Kyle's red and mauve. Each favoured just enough mascara to give him a vaguely piratical look.

And yet in another way — several ways, if he was going to be honest about it — they were unlike any act he'd ever known.

The day was already uncomfortably hot and would only get hotter, but in addition to their usual garb — black Chemical Damage hoodies over tight, skinny-leg Rivet de Cru jeans and Alessandro Dell'Acqua high-top sneakers — they all wore heavy pea coats or parkas. Jake himself favoured a long-haired beaver car coat.

Incredibly, not one of them appeared to sweat. They *never* seemed to sweat.

They were unusual in other ways, too.

As far as he could see, they didn't do drugs, not even the occasional aspirin. Nor did they smoke. And all they ever drank was Barq's root beer. They drank that a lot.

Not that Gerry was complaining. The last thing he needed to be around, now or ever, was booze and drugs. That's what made this gig so perfect for him. But —

Just then Jake climbed back aboard, tall and cadaverous beneath his bulky coat, his black-as-jet eyes hidden behind smoke-grey Hugo Boss sunglasses. He was about twenty-five or so, his long, moody face home to high, well-defined cheekbones and a wide, belligerent mouth above a V-shaped cleft chin.

As his eyes fell to the humming air circulator, he shivered visibly. Then, moving so fast that he was little more than a smudge of motion, he grabbed the fan and ripped it off the dash.

In the same moment he grasped Gerry by one chunky shoulder, dug his fingers hard into the roadie's gaudy Hawaiian shirt and snarled: 'You dumb shit! What'd I tell you about using that thing?'

Gerry shrank back into the corner of his seat, taken aback by the ferocity of the other man's reaction. 'S-sorry, Jake, but it gets so damn' hot — '

'Shut up!' Jake stabbed a finger in Gerry's face. 'I told you that — '

'Yeah, yeah, I know. That's the way you like it.'

'That's right. And what *else* did I tell you?'

As Gerry looked up at him, standing there with his head cocked expectantly to one side, his bullying stance a blatant challenge, he wanted to ask Jake who the fuck he thought he was talking to, but

19

knew he'd lose his job for sure if he did.

'Well?' demanded Jake.

Hating himself for it, Gerry mumbled a response.

'What was that?'

'That you're susceptible to draughts,' Gerry repeated with as much defiance as he thought he could get away with.

'Right.'

'Look, man, I'm sorry — '

Jake leaned forward until they were eyeball to eyeball and spitefully dug his fingers in a little harder as he hissed, 'Sorry doesn't cut it, you dumb fuck!'

Behind his shades, Gerry saw that his eyes had grown near-homicidal.

'You foul up again and I'll kick your fat, sorry ass off this tour,' Jake said. '*Capice?*'

Again Gerry bit off a reply. He was bigger than Jake, bigger than Kyle, Beau and Brad, too, and though he was a peaceable guy, he knew how to handle himself. But he'd always had the damnedest feeling he'd be sorry if he ever tried tangled with these guys. He didn't know why; he just sensed that there was something dangerous about them.

Grudgingly he said: '*Capice.*'

Satisfied, Jake dumped the air circulator into his lap and stalked off to the back of the bus. Gerry watched him go, burning with humiliation.

Still, as much as he'd hated to back down, he knew he had been right to bite his tongue and let them have things their way.

He'd already come close to dying once. He was in no hurry to repeat the experience.

3

When Ed finally regained consciousness, the first thing he became aware of was the silence. It was so complete that at first he thought he'd gone deaf.

He cracked his hazel eyes and flinched at the sunshine slanting into the sickly-hot truck. Slowly, carefully, he sat up and broke the hush with a soft, heartfelt groan.

Scrunch-eyed, he looked around. The truck was a mess. The cab and his lap were covered in heaped sand and broken glass. The road-sign had smashed through the windshield and skewered the back of the passenger seat. He looked at the name printed on it and grunted.

DEAD END
5 ML

He reached up, wincing when he touched the gash in his forehead. It had now scabbed over with blood that was still tacky to the touch. His fingers came away red: he wiped them clean on his tattered pants.

As memory slowly returned, he took several deep breaths and then forced the driver's-side door open. Every inch of him had stiffened up and seemed reluctant to cooperate; as a result he fell more than climbed out. But at least now he could stretch his cramped limbs, brush himself off and check for further injuries.

He was pretty banged up, but didn't think anything was broken.

He'd been lucky. If he'd been anything other than what he was . . .

He reached for his cell phone, flipped it open, realised there was no signal and cursed again. Shoving the phone back into his jacket pocket, he limped to the front of the truck and inspected the damage.

He'd rammed the vehicle into the side of a dune ten or twelve feet high. He realised he was going to have to dig it out again before he could check just how badly the engine, radiator and front axle had been damaged.

Digging was the last thing he felt like doing. He felt lousy. His head ached, his ribs ached, he felt sick and thirsty and just wanted to sleep all the pain away.

But he also wanted to reach Dead End. So he carefully eased off his jacket and threw it into the back of the truck with the rest of his gear. He then climbed up onto the hood, took hold of the road-sign and dragged it back through what was left of the windshield.

Using it as a makeshift shovel, he set about digging the truck out. It was hot work and it played hell with his aches and pains, but having little choice he stuck at it.

After a few minutes, something came free of the loosened sand and rolled against his feet.

It was the last thing he'd expected to see.

It was a human skull.

He jumped back. '*Jesus!*'

It stared back at him, expressionless.

Once he got over the initial shock, his curiosity took over. Propping the road-sign against the truck, he dropped to his knees beside it.

Gingerly he picked it up and turned it

between his fingers. It was cold to the touch and tanned to the colour of old parchment, with heavily-ridged eye sockets above a pear-shaped nasal cavity. The top was scored through here and there, where the plates of the cranium had fused together during its owner's formative years. There were several gaps between the long, stained teeth and no sign of the lower jaw. Neither was there any sign of trauma.

Ed wondered whose skull had it been, and what the hell was it doing out in the middle of nowhere?

Rising, he set it down out of harm's way, deciding that maybe it wasn't such an unusual find after all. Archaeologists were always turning up bones in places like this.

Still, those bones were usually prehistoric. This skull was old, but not *that* old.

He took another look at it. The empty sockets seemed to meet his eyes. Trying to convince himself that it wasn't watching him, he started digging again.

A minute or so later he uncovered the lower jaw.

Then a few chunky vertebrae.

Dry-mouthed now, he set the sign aside once again and started probing more carefully at the loose sand with his fingers, half-dreading what he might find next.

It turned out to be a clavicle.

Then a scattering of ribs.

Then another clavicle followed by what looked suspiciously like a pelvis, scapula and two patellae.

Almost before he knew it, he'd unearthed a sizeable pile of bones of all shapes and sizes, each tanned the same parchment colour as the skull, and all fleshless. They lay in a heap at his feet like the components of some macabre version of pickup sticks.

Spooked, he grabbed the sign, went around to the other side of the truck and began digging out the front tire. He worked for several minutes, making no further discoveries, before finally stopping to catch his breath.

That was when he heard it.

A dry, staccato grating sound . . .

He glanced around. The undulating

desert extended as far as he could see in every direction, wavering in the stifling mid-morning heat. The road, about fifty or sixty yards away, was empty. As best he could tell, he was alone. Neither did he believe that anyone could have snuck up on him unseen.

So what had — ?

He heard it again, except that now it was a soft, sliding kind of sound, like bamboo rubbing against bamboo.

Or bone, whispered a voice in his head, *rubbing against bone*.

He jumped when something scraped against the far side of the truck, something that seemed to first tap and then rake at the fender. Focusing his attention on the spot, he took a step back and raised the road-sign, ready to strike.

'Who's there?' he said.

The only reply was a harsh scraping sound, the sound you get when you claw fingernails down a blackboard. It set his teeth on edge. Tightening his grip on the sign, he repeated: 'Who's there, dammit?'

At last there was movement.

Something began to rise slowly on the

far side of the truck.

From the same spot at which he'd left the piled bones.

It was the skull.

What?

WHAT?

No: he saw almost at once that he was mistaken. But it was an easy mistake to have made.

This wasn't a skull as such, but it was as near as made no difference. It was covered in a thin, drum-tight layer of desiccated, translucent whitish skin. The cheekbones were sharp ridges, the cheeks themselves hollow pits, the narrow jaw-line tapering to a pointed chin from which hung a few greyish whiskers. It wore an old cap or *kepi* atop its long, stringy hair, at the front of which, just above the black brim, two crossed sabres glinted dully in the sunshine.

The figure slowly, painfully continued to claw its way up to its full height — about five-six or -seven, Ed reckoned. Its movements were jerky, badly coordinated.

Beneath the ragged remnants of a dark

blue fatigue jacket with a stand-up collar, its body seemed to be rail-thin, more or less . . . *skeletal*. Its tattered, pale blue pants clung to its skinny waist. Its hands were white, like flour, its fingers long, thin, sharp, with chipped, dirty nails.

But the single most arresting feature was its eyes. They were sunken deep into dark, shadowy sockets, and they looked like dried-out raisins floating in egg-white circles that had somehow turned mouldy over the years.

Ed saw then that the figure was bleeding from the neck and realised that it had been wounded just below the left ear. The parchment skin there looked jagged and torn, and had leaked so much blood that this gaunt stranger was all but drenched in it.

And yet, incredibly, it still lived.

Even as Ed watched, the figure — *soldier*, he corrected himself subconsciously, for the blue jacket and pants were obviously parts of a uniform — opened its mouth as if intending to speak. As its thin, translucent lips peeled back, he saw several gaps between the figure's long, stained teeth.

Just like those in the skull he'd found.

And in the same moment that he finally made the connection between the two, an impossible connection he knew he'd been trying not to make, a strong wind sprang up from out of nowhere, whisking dust into a gauzy, spiralling curtain around him.

He narrowed his eyes against it, slowly shaking his head in denial because he knew he had to be mistaken. The wind quickly gathered in strength, buffeted him back a yard or so and then started roaring ever louder in his ears as the churned-up sand began to flense his skin.

He closed his eyes and mouth tight against it, dropped the sign so that he could clap his hands over his ears and blot out the worst of its banshee wail until —

Until —

Silence.

Abruptly the wind stopped, dying down as quickly as it had blown up, and when he opened his eyes again and took his hands away from his ears he saw that everything was as it had been just seconds earlier: calm, peaceful.

And he was alone.

There was no sign of the wounded soldier.

He snatched up the road-sign again, hurried around the truck, stopped and hitched a breath when he saw nothing there save the pickup stick bones he'd unearthed, piled exactly where he'd left them.

He scanned the sand around them, but the only tracks he found were his own.

Confused, he sagged against the truck's hot bodywork and told himself that he must have imagined the entire episode. It was the only answer that made any sense. The bump to his head, the effort of digging in this heat . . . they'd conspired to play a trick on him.

But what a trick.

Christ.

For a long moment he just stood there, breathing hard, positive that he'd hallucinated. And yet still there remained a single nagging doubt. Why hallucinate about some old-time soldier, of all things?

Hell, if it came to that, why did anyone

hallucinate about anything?

He released a breath, fully expecting his unease to fade. Instead it grew stronger. With effort he gathered his wits and was about to continue digging when instead, acting on a sudden, inexplicable impulse, he decided to examine the truck's fender more closely.

He knelt.

Looked.

Went cold.

Up close he could just about discern four long, almost invisible scratches in the paintwork, as if something had indeed clawed its way up the side of the vehicle.

A soft, sliding *kind of sound*, he remembered. *Like bamboo rubbing against bamboo.*

Or bone rubbing against bone.

Thoughtfully he glanced back over his shoulder at the piled bones, at the skull crowning them.

And again:

A harsh scraping sound, the sound you get when you claw fingernails down a blackboard.

Hesitantly he reached out and ran his

fingertips across the faint scratches. The metal was cold to the touch, so cold in fact that when he looked closer, he saw that a thin film of condensation had formed around them.

He hadn't noticed them before, and didn't believe they could have happened during the crash. So what explanation did that leave, apart from the impossible one?

In the distance, something growled.

Forgetting his assorted hurts, he leapt up and spun around —

He was still alone.

But the growling continued.

He turned toward the highway, raised his hand to shield his eyes from the sun-glare and after a few seconds spotted a bulky, red-orange shape chugging toward him from the south.

At the same moment he realised that the sound he'd heard was the uneven growl of its diesel engine.

Relieved, he jogged stiffly toward the highway, waving both arms above his head. As he drew closer he saw that the approaching vehicle was a tractor.

'Hey!' he yelled. 'Hey, over here!'

But the driver had already seen him. He brought the tractor to a gear-grinding halt. It was a fifty year-old Case 500 that reeked of oil and diesel. A pink parasol that was easily as old as the tractor had been rigged up to shade the driver, an Apache Indian who appeared to be older than the tractor and the parasol put together.

The newcomer wore a beaded buckskin vest over a creased blue shirt. He wore the shirt outside an old pair of black jeans that were tucked into soft, shin-high moccasins. He was short, stocky and thickening around the middle.

'Boy, am I glad to see you,' Ed said.

The old Apache stared at him through dark, unreadable eyes. Deeply etched wrinkles had turned his round, cinnamon-coloured face into a relief map. They scored his forehead from east-to-west and slashed his cheeks from north-to-south. They gathered at the corners of his pouchy eyes and the unsmiling, almost lipless tear of his mouth, so that now, in his autumn years, he looked more as if he'd been carved from wood than born of woman.

His shoulder-length hair — dust-grey shot through with the occasional blue-black strand — hung dry and lifeless from beneath his black Stetson. The Stetson, Ed noted, was especially cool: it had a rattlesnake band from behind which poked a single owl feather.

'I wrecked my truck,' Ed explained. 'Couldn't get a signal on my phone to call for help.'

The Apache blinked slowly, once.

'Thought maybe you'd tow me into Dead End.'

When the Apache continued to stare at him, Ed wondered if he could speak or understand English. He was about to repeat everything when the old Apache looked off across the desert to where Ed's truck sat nose-deep in the dune.

'Can do,' he said.

It quickly became obvious that he'd had done this kind of thing before, because he made slow but efficient work of it. He drove the tractor over to the truck, backed it up to within a few yards and rummaged around in the oily tool chest behind the seat until he produced a length of chain. He stared at the bones a few times while he strung the chain from the tractor's hitch to the truck's tow-bar, but made no comment.

Once they'd hauled the truck free, he indicated for Ed to join him on the narrow space behind the tractor seat. As soon as Ed was safely aboard the Apache gunned his scratchy six-cylinder engine and they chug-chugged back to the highway, the truck wobbling along behind them.

Rocking to and fro behind his silent companion, Ed gratefully closed his eyes. All at once his weariness caught up with him. The tractor continued to roll along beneath them, its gentle see-saw motion lulling him into a doze.

In his mind he saw Dead End's narrow, tree-lined main street unfolding before him. It looked curiously old-fashioned. There were no modern buildings to be seen, not even any sidewalks, just two ragged lines of single-storey, whitewashed adobes and the occasional plank-built, high-fronted store.

He ran curious eyes across each basic,

hand-painted sign in turn. *BARBER-SHOP . . . LIVERY . . . FEED AND GRAIN . . . WHEELWRIGHT . . . DRY GOODS . . . BILLIARD HALL . . . J D RESTAURANT . . . BEER — EATS*.

He looked all around him and realised the street was empty of traffic.

But it was *littered* with bodies.

He started to say something. But the old Apache had vanished and taken his tractor with him. Ed was all alone on the heat-hammered street, confused and spooked.

Everywhere he looked he saw the dead and the dying. They lay in the street or propped against mesquite trees, hitch-racks, horse-troughs and storefronts; whiskery men in homespun shirts and dirt-caked brogans; children with dark, dried blood crusting their nostrils; women of all ages in crinolines and calico that was now stained with puke and faeces.

He asked himself what the hell was going on. Shawls, bonnets, claw-hammer coats — these people, these bloated, dark-skinned bodies were dressed in the kind of clothes you'd normally see on reruns of *Gunsmoke* or *The High Chaparral*.

It didn't make any sense.

But before he could consider the matter further, he caught sight of a horse-drawn freight wagon parked up ahead on his right, and his blood ran cold.

A handful of soldiers dressed in the same tattered blue as the skeletal soldier he'd seen back in the desert were collecting up the dead and tossing them into the back of the wagon. There were already so many bodies piled in the wagon-bed that it was riding low on its chassis.

Noticing that the soldiers wore neckerchiefs tied over their noses and mouths, Ed suddenly became aware of a thick, cloying putrescence permeating the warm air. As the noxious stench of voided bowels and puddled spew flooded his senses, he almost gagged.

Then a movement on the other side of the street distracted him.

A skinny, wispy-bearded man in his forties had stumbled out of a store and now began to stagger across the street, holding a canteen at arm's length and upside-down to show that it was empty. He wore a sweat-stained grey shirt and high-waisted grey striped pants that were held up by wide red gallowses. A black slouch hat sat atop his head.

The soldiers stopped what they were doing and turned to face him. One of them, the twin yellow stripes on his sleeves identifying him as a corporal, held up his right hand and shouted something. But curiously, Ed couldn't hear what he said.

He couldn't hear *anything*.

Ignoring the corporal, the skinny man kept staggering forward. His skin was chalky and dry, his dark eyes glazed and bloodshot. It was clear from the way he kept grabbing his stomach and hunching up that he was in great physical distress.

The soldiers, watching him approach, exchanged uneasy glances. They were scared, and Ed didn't blame them. Clearly there was contagion here, and they had to do whatever it took to minimise the risk to their lives.

The corporal yelled again. To Ed it was like watching a silent movie. He willed the civilian to stay where he was or go back where he'd come from, but the man kept on coming.

One of the soldiers turned and dragged some kind of antique, breech-loading rifle from the back of the wagon. He brought it to his shoulder and took aim. The corporal yelled again, gesturing that the man should turn back, or else.

Still the man ignored him.

A second later smoke billowed from the carbine at the soldier's shoulder. The bullet tore into the sick man's chest and ripped a meaty exit hole out through his spine. He went limp, stumbled back and collapsed on the dirt.

He landed beside the body of a young blonde in a red and black satin dress. A single streak of pure white hair swept back from the girl's left temple. But that wasn't what caught Ed's attention.

It was her throat . . .

Oh my God . . .

At her throat was the same ragged wound that Ed had seen on the man in his hallucination.

Seeing her twitch as the dead man collapsed beside her, and realising that she was still alive, the corporal snapped out some orders and the soldier quickly reloaded his carbine: Ed saw an empty brass cartridge flip and spin from the top of the weapon, saw the soldier thumb in a fresh round.

He came a few paces closer, until he was standing over the girl, aiming the carbine right at her face, and Ed thought helplessly, *Oh no, he's going to finish her, he's going to shoot her in cold blood —*

And in the very next instant —

BANG!

He jerked awake, gasping and sweating hard.

Heart pounding, he realised that he had fallen asleep; that he'd been dreaming and the sound he'd mistaken for a gunshot was actually the old tractor's engine backfiring.

He sagged with relief and wiped the sweat from his brow.

'Buy a hat,' said the old Apache, looking back at him. 'Sun's hot enough to boil your brains.'

Ed licked his lips, still struggling to make the transition from sleep to waking. 'I don't plan on hanging around that long.'

The old Apache arched one eyebrow. 'No?'

Ed frowned.

The way the Indian had said the word implied that he knew better.

4

About half an hour later the desert finally gave way to a lush green stand of mesquite, juniper trees, desert fern and willow. A sign on their right said:

**WELCOME TO DEAD END
(FORMERLY SILVERTON)
COFFIN COUNTY, AZ
FOUNDED 1881**

To Ed's relief, the town that shortly came into sight beyond the trees looked nothing like the one in his dream. The broad Main Street curved gently left between two rows of square, flat-roofed stores, cafés, markets and mercantiles. Trucks and cars were parked along its entire length, and the sidewalks were bustling.

They passed a movie theatre, a big, stone structure set back from the main drag that the Apache identified as the

Dead End Clubhouse and Memorial Library, and as Main straightened out again he spotted a pool hall and service station, an ice plant, volunteer fire station and the antiquated offices of the Dead End *Weekly Monitor*.

Why anyone would want to change the name of the place from Silverton to Dead End was a mystery to him. As near as he could see, the name in no way reflected the town. He picked out a neat park surrounded by tall cypress trees, at the centre of which stood a picturesque gazebo; newspaper dispensers stocked with copies of *USA Today*; a notice board outside the quaint town hall advertising dances at the Clubhouse and details of the Property Watch Program. It was typical small-town America, and he liked what he saw.

But then his grin faded, for in among the townsfolk going about their business on the sidewalks he noticed other, more curious figures: a tall man dressed in black with silver spurs at his heels and a curl-brimmed black hat not unlike that worn by the Apache; another in a smart pale grey suit, the jacket cut more like an old-time frock coat, with a distinctive bed-of-flowers vest and a black four-in-hand tie.

He, like the others of his kind, wore trendy wraparound sun-glasses, and for headgear he favoured an old-fashioned flat black coachman's hat.

These and others like them, both men and long-skirted, bonneted women, looked so out-of-place among the rest of the population that they were hard to miss.

'You folks re-enact the Old West for the tourists around here, Chief?' Ed asked above the choking cough of the old tractor engine.

'The Settlers, you mean?'

'Is that what you call 'em?'

'That's what they call themselves.'

'Who are they?'

'Religious folks, they say — people who cling to the old ways. Like the Amish.'

'Are there many of 'em?'

'Enough.'

Sensing that the Indian did not want to discuss the subject, Ed said, 'Pull into the first garage you come to, okay?'

'Want my advice?'

'Sure.'

'Stop at a bar first. You're dehydrated. Need a drink.'

'What I *need* is to get my truck fixed.'

'Impatience,' said the Apache, 'is a white man's invention.'

'So is the radiator, and right now mine's got more holes than Swiss cheese.'

The Apache shrugged, and pulled in at the first garage they came to.

Hearing the tractor roll up onto his forecourt, the owner of the place slid out from beneath a massive yellow and white Mack CH613 and wiped his big hands on an oily rag. As he stood up, Ed saw with surprise that he was a Settler too. Apparently they didn't *all* cling to the old ways, then: leastways not if they wanted to make a buck.

The Settler, a broad-chested man of about forty, introduced himself as Charlie Steelgood. He wore the apparently obligatory wraparound sunglasses and a Yuma Scorpions baseball cap pulled down over his long, uncombed brown hair. He had a flat, broken nose, a fuzzy untrimmed beard the colour of freshly-turned dirt, and in his worn leather bib apron, collarless off-white shirt and sturdy burgundy cotton pants, he looked more like an old-time blacksmith than a mechanic.

Without asking, he inspected the truck and told Ed that it would take two or three days to get a new radiator from Tucson. When Ed repeated the verdict to the Apache, the Indian's dark eyes glinted with amusement.

'Plenty of time now to buy that hat.'

Ed grinned and reached into his pocket. 'Thanks for the ride, chief.'

The Indian glanced at the bill Ed pressed into his hand and raised his eyebrows. 'Andrew Jackson. My lucky day.'

'The luck was all mine. If you hadn't come along when you did — '

'Not luck,' the Apache corrected. 'I was expecting you.'

'Expecting me? Chief, how the hell —?'

'I am shaman, not chief.'

Before Ed could reply, the Indian put the tractor in gear and chugged across the forecourt, out onto Main.

Ed gathered his gear from the truck. Although his ribs were still sore, his headache had eased a little and he figured some food might finish it off for good. He headed for the café across the street.

Behind his sunglasses, Charlie Steelgood watched him dodge traffic, the expression on his pale, jowly face at once curious and troubled.

During his inspection of the truck he'd seen the books spilled across the passenger seat, and wondered what a man like Ed was doing with them.

He reckoned the colonel would wonder the same thing.

* * *

The lunchtime trade had more or less been and gone by now, and the café — *Wanda's* — was quiet but for a radio playing soft rock in the background.

As Ed entered he saw that the only other patron was a beefy trucker at the far end of the counter, working his way through a Philly cheesesteak and fries. Ed dropped into a booth near the door and studied the menu.

'Hey, Wanda,' the trucker called. 'How 'bout you get off your cute little butt and gimme a refill?'

The waitress, who was also the owner, stubbed out her cigarette in an ashtray and slid off her stool beside the cash register. 'Sure.'

Ed glanced at her. Her long, buttery yellow hair was pulled over to the left side of her head in a ponytail that hung forward across her left shoulder. A little below average height, he noticed she had an exceptional body beneath her tight white tank-top, skinny-leg jeans and Nikes. She wore a short green denim apron around her slim waist and he guessed she was around twenty-five.

As she refilled the trucker's cup, she muttered, 'Crazy damn' heat. I go to bed early and still wake up bushed.'

'Maybe you should try goin' to bed *alone* for a change,' grinned the trucker. He was a big-bellied man of about thirty, with a round, florid face and fleshy lips, tired-looking, red-rimmed blue eyes and a weak, bristly jaw.

'Much as I hate to spoil your fantasies, Dale,' she said, 'I'm too tired to even screw around these days.'

She put the pot back on the hotplate and stretched. As she pushed her ponytail aside to rub her neck, the trucker saw something that made him grin even wider.

'If you're sleepin' alone, baby, who's givin' you love bites?'

Wanda quickly pulled her dangling ponytail over her neck again. 'Mosquitoes, you smart-ass.'

'Well, I'd sure like to be one o' them mosquitoes,' he leered.

'Be careful what you wish for, honey.'

She came around the counter and across the checked floor to Ed's booth. She was sexy more than pretty with big deep-set blue eyes, a snub nose, pouting lips and a strong chin. Looking at her, Ed noticed a single streak of white hair sweeping back from her left temple. It stirred a vague half-memory in him that he couldn't quite pull into focus.

''Afternoon, hon'. What can I get you besides coffee?'

'Is the lobster fresh?' he asked, deadpan.

'Flown in this mornin' from Maine.'

'I'll take it. And a glass of chilled Chardonnay.'

Wanda chuckled. 'One blue plate special and a cold Bud comin' up,' she yelled to the cook.

After she served Ed the meatloaf, gravy and mashed potatoes, she returned to her stool at the counter and lit another cigarette. The trucker paid for his meal, stifled a belch and left, promising to come back and see her again real soon.

Wanda swivelled her stool around and looked at Ed. 'Were you ever a trucker, hon'?'

'Nope.'

'Didn't think so. You been a waitress as long as me, you get so you can pick out a trucker in a crowd. Not that Dale isn't a nice guy, you understand. It's just he can get on your nerves after a while.'

Ed didn't say anything. But as he went on eating he felt Wanda's eyes on him and wondered if she thought she knew him from somewhere.

'That's a nasty-lookin' cut you got there,' she said after a little. 'Could use some stitches.'

'I'll live. But I'd be obliged if you could point me to a decent motel.'

'All the motels around here went belly-up years ago. But there's a hotel, half a block up. The Vickers House. You can't miss it.' She lit a fresh cigarette, inhaled deeply before saying: 'Where you from?'

'San Francisco.'

'You're a long way from home.'

'I'm on vacation.'

'*Here?*'

'Why not?'

She shrugged. 'No reason, I guess. It's just that this ain't exactly the Garden Spot of Arizona. Other than truckers, the only folks who usually pass through Dead End are tourists who've lost their way. And honey, you don't look like no tourist.'

'I collect arrowheads,' Ed said. 'Sort of a hobby. I heard there used to be Apaches in these parts and thought I'd take a look around, maybe do a little digging.'

'Well, you're right about the Apaches. Chiricahua and Mescalero, mostly, and a few White Mountain. If you want to know about Apaches, you should talk to Sam Cocheta. He grew up here.'

'Who's Sam Cocheta?'

She smiled. 'One of our local, uh, 'characters.''

'He own a tractor, by any chance?'

'You *know* him?'

'He towed me here after I wrecked my truck. Told me to buy a hat.'

'You're lucky he didn't ask you to buy him a *drink*.'

'He did that too.'

They were both laughing when the bell over the door tinkled and a tall woman in a chocolate brown pantsuit over a pale yellow t-shirt entered. She glanced questioningly at them, wondering if she'd interrupted something until Wanda said, 'Good timing, Fiona. I was just telling Handsome here that he needs to get that cut stitched.'

Turning to Ed, the woman treated him to a frank, brown-eyed examination. He squirmed a little. She was a year or so older than Wanda, with short, shag-cut black hair softened by dark red highlights that tumbled from her crown and lightened the fringe that had been cut to fall slantwise across her high, clear forehead. Her face was oval, almost angular, with good cheekbones and a straight nose.

'Come by my office later,' she told him, 'and I'll take care of it.'

'You're a doctor?'

'Doctor, librarian, council member. You name it and I'm usually involved in it somewhere.'

'Underachiever, huh?'

She smiled, revealing strong white teeth, and thrust out her right hand. 'Fiona Vickers. Pleased to meet you.'

He rose from the table. 'Ed Knight. Likewise.' Her palm was cool, her grip firm and confident. 'Vickers?' he repeated. 'You don't happen to run the hotel as well, do you?'

'No, that's my father's province.'

'Ah. So between you, you've got Dead End all sewn up.'

'Something like that.'

'Then it looks as if I'll be paying you both a visit later today.'

'Well, I can't speak for my dad, but I'll certainly be looking forward to it.'

He'd forgotten he was still holding her hand, and was almost sorry when she finally pulled it away and turned back to Wanda. 'Fix me some iced tea to go, will you?'

'Comin' right up.'

* * *

The Vickers House proved to be an ugly cube of a building three stories high and sheathed in brown sandstone. Oriel windows, each one supported from beneath by ornamental black ironwork, overlooked the quiet side street it dominated, and a small, ugly gargoyle — it looked to Ed like a cross between an ape and a dog with bat's wings spread wide — perched on the red-brick lintel over the double doors.

Entering the hotel he found the panelled lobby more welcoming. There was a highly-polished key rack and a pigeonhole for mail behind the orderly cherry wood counter, and soft Berber carpet the colour of almonds underfoot.

Ed asked the man behind the front desk for a room facing the street for two, maybe three nights.

'Room's cheaper by the week, son,' Max Vickers replied, pausing before swiping Ed's credit card through the reader.

'I don't plan on staying that long.'

'Sure?'

'Well, not unless you know something I don't?'

Max smiled. He was a slightly-built, well-preserved sixty year-old with short, mid-brown hair that was thinning on top, and which gave him an unusually high forehead above ice-blue eyes and a smile that seemed to sit uneasily on his narrow lips.

'No secrets in Dead End, Mr Knight,' he said.

'In other words, you're saying my radiator will take a week to get here?'

'If you're lucky.'

'Great.'

'Oh, don't worry. Folks hereabouts are real neighbourly. They go out of their way to make strangers feel welcome. The time'll fly.'

Ed's expression, as he took his key and headed for the elevator, indicated that he doubted that very much.

Max thoughtfully watched him go.

The room was clean, spacious and frankly much better than Ed had been expecting. He stowed his gear in the corner, figuring it wasn't worth the bother of unpacking. Then stripping down he entered the bathroom and showered. The hot water made the gash on his forehead sting. Drying off, he checked it in the mirror. Wanda was right, he decided — he did need to get it seen to. Besides, it was a good excuse to see Fiona again.

He changed into a clean white shirt and jeans, got directions to Fiona's office from her father and fifteen minutes later was sitting on her examination table, trying to focus on an *Understanding Cholesterol* poster on the opposite wall as Fiona finished stitching the wound.

'There,' she said finally. 'That should do it.'

'Thanks. How much do I owe you?'

She dropped needle and suture thread into a kidney dish and took it to the small corner sink. 'It's on the house.'

'Thanks, but I always pay my way.'

As she peeled off her latex gloves, she eyed him thoughtfully. 'Do you suffer from any chronic illnesses?' she asked suddenly.

'Not that I know of. Why?'

'Diabetes, asthma, allergies?'

'Nope.'

'High or low blood pressure?'

'What *is* this, Doc?'

'Have you given blood within the last two months?'

'No.'

'Know what blood-type you are?'

'AB Positive.'

'All right,' she said. 'Roll up your sleeve.'

'*What?*'

'You want to pay your way, don't you? Well, we can always use blood. Donate a pint and we'll call it even.'

'Fair enough.' He stretched out on the table. She went to work quickly and efficiently, and after he was rigged up, gave him a soft ball and told him to start squeezing.

'What's wrong?' she asked when he kept looking at her.

'I was just thinking.'

'About . . . ?'

'You. This place.'

'What about it?'

'Doesn't make sense.'

'Sure it does. Not every doctor dreams of getting rich in the big city, you know.'

'Then I guess I've met the wrong doctors.' He glanced around the office and spotted a black bag on a chair beside her cluttered desk. 'Man, don't tell me you make house-calls as well?'

'All the time. I may be old-fashioned, but I believe that's what being a doctor's all about — helping the sick regardless of where they live or whether or not they're covered by Blue Cross.'

'Very noble.'

She arched one dark eyebrow. 'Are you by any chance being sarcastic, Mr Knight?'

'Uh-uh. I really mean it.'

About ten minutes later she removed the needle, stuck a Band-Aid over the wound and then handed him a bottle of water and a candy bar. 'Here, take these. And don't do anything vigorous for a while.'

'Anything?' he repeated.

She caught his meaning at once and smiled. 'Anything.'

'Well, if you say so. But tell me something.'

'Sure.'

'If I should feel a little light-headed later on, can I call on you for some personal TLC?'

Fiona cocked her head at him. 'Are you asking me out?'

'Well . . . '

'You move right along, don't you?'

'Is that a yes?'

When she didn't reply immediately, he urged her to, 'Go on, take a chance. You never know, maybe there's a prince hiding under this rough exterior.'

She studied him a moment longer, then handed him a business card. 'Just so long as it's not a frog,' she replied.

5

Just before sunset Wanda closed the café, put the money and receipts in the safe and locked up behind her. Across the road, she saw Dale White and Charlie Steelgood on Charlie's garage forecourt, standing beside Dale's big yellow and white Mack truck and trailer. Charlie was pointing to this and that as he explained the work he'd carried out on the vehicle. Dale nodded to show he understood and both men went into Charlie's office to settle the bill.

Realising she didn't have much time, Wanda hurried off.

* * *

Sam Cocheta sat in a rocking chair outside a small adobe structure on the outskirts of town, slowly working his way through a bottle of Old Crustacean. Away to the west the sun was balancing

61

on the jagged horizon and all around him purple shadows were stretching long toward night.

Any way you cut it Sam's front yard was a mess, dominated by his old tractor and all the paraphernalia needed to keep it running. Though the sign over the door read *TRADING POST*, it was clear that he hadn't done much in the way of trading for some time. It wasn't surprising. His stock consisted of old Apache-weave baskets and handmade arrows, Kachina dolls and medicine wheels, dream-catchers, moccasins, saddle purses and dye charts — all mostly worthless.

Sometimes Sam felt pretty much the same way.

He had no true idea how old he was. He had a vague notion that he was close to ninety, but he didn't *feel* ninety, so maybe he was mistaken.

As for worthless . . .

Well, he'd known that feeling for more years than he cared to count. His surname, Cocheta, was the Apache word for *unknown*, and it was a good name for there was much about him that was exactly that. And yet he had known practically his entire life the one single purpose for which he had been born.

The problem was that he had spent — wasted — that life just waiting to carry it out.

Until now.

Now, he felt strongly that the waiting was almost over. He drank to that knowledge, for he had always harboured a secret fear that he would die before he could fulfil his destiny.

A little later Dale White's distinctive eighteen-wheeler came barrelling out of town. Seeing Sam, Dale gave a blast on his air-horn that tore the dusk apart. Sam raised his barley wine in toast as the truck swept past, the slipstream of its passage stirring the owl feather stuck in his rattlesnake hatband.

But as he watched the truck shrink into the fading amber distance, new lines suddenly joined those already etched deep into his forehead.

It was true. The time of waiting *was* almost over.

Yet he somehow knew that before the

final reckoning, there would be blood-shed. A lot of it.

And he had a very bad feeling that it was going to start with Dale White.

★ ★ ★

A mile outside town, Dale spotted someone walking alongside the two-lane highway some fifty yards ahead. He hunched forward over the wheel, squinting in the twilight to make sure his eyes weren't playing tricks on him.

His headlights picked out a blonde girl with her back to him, wearing some kind of red satin party dress with a black lace fringe.

Even in the fading light he could see she had a hot body with great legs sheathed in black lace stockings, her feet strapped into highly impractical but oh-so-sexy high-heeled ankle boots. A single red feather was clipped in her lustrous, free-flowing hair.

He had watched so many westerns on TV that she immediately reminded him of an old-time saloon girl.

Slowing down, he pulled alongside her and leaned out the cab window. 'Hey, baby. Where's the costume party?'

She stopped and looked up at him.

'Hello, Dale,' she said.

Surprised, he nudged his cap back. 'Wanda! What the hell you doin' way out here?'

She smiled suggestively. 'Hopin' to run into someone like you.'

The compliment took Dale by surprise. He gave an awkward, embarrassed shrug, thinking she was joshing with him, as so many women did.

He didn't kid himself. He'd never been attractive to the opposite sex — he was too fat, for one thing; he drank too much, smoked too much and his job as a long-hauler meant that home was and always would be just a place he occasionally passed through.

Of course, he usually managed to hide his low self-esteem by cracking wise. A man could cover a multitude of uncertainties that way, and sometimes, if he was lucky, even ease a little of the loneliness that was always at his core.

But flirting was one thing. If he didn't know better, he'd say that right now, Wanda was hitting on him.

'Y-You wanna ride?' he asked hesitantly.

'What do you think?'

There was no missing the suggestiveness in her voice. Dale grinned, barely able to believe his good fortune. 'Then climb on in, baby.'

She smelled of jasmine and orange blossom, sandalwood and bergamot, and as soon as her perfume filled the cab he was completely and hopelessly intoxicated by her.

As she settled herself beside him, she said that she knew a place where they could go and have a good time and not be interrupted. He'd heard her say those exact same words plenty of times in his fantasies, but never expected to hear them for real.

He set the hammer down and got them moving again, and was just about to ask for directions when she reached over and grabbed his crotch.

Oh man.

He kept staring straight through the windshield while she unzipped him and then buried her face in his lap. The truck veered ever so slightly to the right, then came back into line.

'Where, uh . . . where we goin', then, Wanda?' His voice was a high, breathless choke.

She stopped what she was doing long enough to say, 'There's a sign up ahead. Follow it.'

No longer able to think straight, Dale kept the truck surging forward, but it was hard to hold to a steady speed. Sometimes he'd slow to a crawl only to accelerate again as she brought him ever closer to orgasm. His head spun, his pulses throbbed. He told himself this wasn't happening, that it *couldn't* be happening . . .

And yet it was!

Shortly he spotted the sign she'd told him about.

OLD SILVER MINES
ALT. RTE
3 ML

He swapped the highway for a narrow dirt road. It was full dark now and his headlights showed that they were following a winding trail between manzanita- and fernbush-covered slopes crowned by the tortured silhouettes of twisted madroño trees.

'Where — uh — where exactly are we — uh — goin', baby?'

Without looking up, Wanda said huskily: 'I'm takin' you to paradise, Dale.'

He wished she'd be a little more specific. But by now he was hers to command, so he just continued to follow the old dirt road until at last it came to a rocky hillside and a second sign that read:

DANGER!
PRIVATE PROPERTY!
KEEP OUT!

Just before he braked and killed the big E7 engine, he saw that they'd stopped on a cleared patch of ground in front of a roughly square, timber-supported mine entrance. The next thing he knew, she'd zipped him up and jumped out of the cab into the darkness. He eagerly followed her, hesitating only briefly when he saw the sign.

'Don't worry about that,' she told him. 'It's only there to keep the tourists away.'

He sensed more than saw her move in the shadows, then felt her hand squeeze gently at his crotch.

'Come on, honey,' she whispered.

Taking his hand, she headed for the mine entrance and he followed her with neither pause nor question. A crude infra-red lighting system ran along the centre of the tunnel roof that had the curious effect of making the tunnel seem darker than if it hadn't been lit at all. If Dale noticed it, however, he paid it no mind. His attention was even more firmly focused on Wanda and he was finding it increasingly difficult to curb his growing impatience.

They followed the tunnel for twenty or thirty yards. The floor was sandy, uneven, the walls rough, grey and broken every few yards by splintery, dried-out timber supports.

'Hey, baby,' he said, stopping and

pulling her toward him, 'how about some more pre-game warm-up, huh?'

She responded by kissing him hard and deep, grabbing the back of his head and pulling his lips against hers. It was a long passionate kiss, filled with a wild sense of abandonment that he'd never known before, and he responded accordingly.

Even when they finally came up for air, the passion stayed with her and she leaned back against the tunnel wall, tugged the front of her dress lower and pulled his face down to the inviting valley between her breasts.

He went eagerly, kissing, biting, nuzzling, until —

— until he heard a fluttering of wings somewhere off in the distance.

From some place deeper within the mine.

It was an eerie sound and though he did not want to stop kissing her breasts, he felt an uneasy chill pass through him and he reluctantly pulled himself away from her. As he glanced about him he muttered: 'What the fuck is that?'

But deep down he already knew what it

was. Bats! Bats that had been disturbed by their presence. And by the increasingly frantic, papery rush of their wings he knew the creatures were getting out of there, fast.

'We better take cover, Wanda,' he said.

She made no reply.

The sound was building to a roar now, as the bats came surging along the tunnel, closer, closer, closer —

'Wanda?' he said again, turning back to her.

Except that she wasn't Wanda anymore; at least not the Wanda whose tongue had just been probing in his mouth.

This Wanda's blue eyes had turned red, the pupils had somehow thinned and elongated to black elliptical slits, her skin had whitened and dried out over her skull, and as she opened her mouth —

Oh Jesus.

In the next instant she blurred forward and sunk sharp, overlarge canines into his throat. Pain seared through him as she shook her head back and forth, viciously, like a terrier intent on breaking the neck of a rat.

As the rushing of wings finally reached its crescendo, Dale White screamed.

It was the sound he took with him into eternity.

★ ★ ★

Ed dug Fiona's business card out of his shirt pocket, studied it a moment and then thumbed her number into his cell phone. The line rang a few times and then Fiona said, 'Yes, hello?'

'Fiona? Hi. It's Ed Knight.'

There was a brief silence. 'Oh, hi, Ed. What can I do for you?'

'I was hoping you might administer some of that TLC you promised me earlier.'

He heard the smile in her voice. 'Well, I don't exactly remember promising it.'

'Too bad, because I sure need it right now. Giving you all that blood this afternoon has left me ravenous.'

'So what's the problem?'

'I hate to eat alone.'

'Ah. So you want company, is that it?'

'Not just *any* company.'

'What did you have in mind?'

'How about you tell me the name of Dead End's swankiest restaurant and I meet you there in say, half an hour?'

'Well,' she said after a pause, 'if you think it'll help . . . '

'Oh, it will. Definitely. In fact, I feel better already just knowing you're about to say yes.'

She laughed. 'Okay, smooth talker. We'll try *Le Cruset*, on the corner of Fifth and Main. I hear their parmentier with duck, *foie gras* and truffles is to die for.'

'Sounds — '

' — expensive?'

'Perfect,' he said. 'I'll meet you there in thirty minutes.'

He was just ending the call when a text came in. He opened it and read:

Arrive sometime tomorrow.

His jaw tightened. It was the best news he'd had all day.

* * *

Shortly after Ed left for his date with Fiona, two bright headlights washed across the front of the hotel. Moments later a long, silver-white tour bus with flush black privacy windows drew up outside. Emblazoned along the side of the bus was the legend *PLATINUM DEAD*.

With his usual mix of slouch and swagger, Jake Simms led the rest of the band down the steps, across the sidewalk and into the hotel. Max, about to go off duty, saw them enter and immediately turned on a professional greeting smile.

'Good evening. Welcome to the Vickers House.'

Jake raked his fingers up through his long, streaked black hair. He was chewing gum, his head nodding to some rhythm that only he could hear as he threw a disdainful glance around the lobby. 'We're the *Platinum Dead*,' he said.

Max checked the register. 'We've been expecting you. Here for one week, right?'

'Maybe longer. Depends on how it goes.'

'We're working on songs for our new album,' explained Brad. He was about a head shorter than Jake, but it was impossible to judge his build because of the heavy jacket he — and the others — wore buttoned to the throat. 'Hopin' to get inspiration from the desert.'

The door opened again and the band's roadie, a fat, bearded man in a light blue Hawaiian shirt, struggled inside. He was sweating heavily and apparently trying to break the world record for how many bags a single man could carry at one time.

'Gerry'll sign us in,' said Jake.

Max nodded, handed out keys and said, 'Third floor at the end of the hall.'

As the band entered the elevator, Gerry Irwin dropped the bags and fished a credit card from his wallet. 'Doesn't it ever cool down around here?' he griped.

'Not until winter,' Max said. 'But don't worry. All the rooms are air-conditioned.'

'Then I hope it can be turned off.'

'Who'd want to do that?'

Gerry nodded toward the elevator, just as the doors closed. 'They would,' he grumbled. 'Crazy bastards, they feel the cold like no-one I've ever known. I tell you, mister, if you can't switch that air conditioning off, then you'd better make damn' sure you switch your heating system on.'

* * *

As they came to the end of the meal, Ed smiled across at Fiona and said, 'So what's the verdict: am I a frog or a prince?'

She returned his smile and treated him to another of her frank examinations. 'Still too early to tell,' she said. 'But if it's any consolation, I'm leaning toward prince. Problem is, Dead End is about as short on princes as it is on frogs, so I'm having trouble finding comparisons.'

'There's hope for me yet, then?'

'There's *always* hope.'

'Spoken like a true physician.'

He took a sip from his glass. He'd ordered a 2004 Grignolino port, a choice that impressed her. 'That reminds me,' he said. 'I checked Dead End out on the internet. They said it used to be a mining town, but didn't say why the name was changed from Silverton.'

Her face clouded. 'There was a cholera epidemic back in eighteen-eighty-something. It almost wiped out the entire population. The town only had one doctor, and he was so swamped that a lot of people ended up dying in the street.'

Remembering his dream, Ed's good mood suddenly evaporated.

The street was empty of traffic.
But it was fairly littered with bodies.

'The army was called in to help bury the dead,' she continued, unaware of the change in him.

A handful of soldiers dressed in the same tattered blue as the man/thing he'd seen back in the desert were collecting up the dead and tossing them into the back of the wagon.

'But there were so many contagious bodies that the soldiers got scared and ended up burning them instead.'

Keeping his voice casual, he said,

'What did they, uh, do with all the bones?'

'No-one knows for sure. But the Apaches believe they were thrown down the mine-shaft, forcing their spirits to haunt the earth forever.'

Not all the bones, he told himself, thinking about what he'd unearthed around the dune earlier that morning.

'After that,' she went on, 'the Indians called the town 'The Place Where Graves Have Ended.' Years later it was shortened to Graves' End. And then, later still, it was changed by some unknown character — probably an undertaker with a warped sense of humour — to Dead End.'

They both laughed, and doing his best to shrug off his disquiet Ed said, 'Is it the wine, or am I really having this much fun?'

When Fiona looked into his eyes he had the craziest feeling that the world had suddenly stopped turning. After a long, thoughtful moment she said softly, 'It's not the wine.'

★　★　★

Deep at the heart of the played-out mine, the long, often-labyrinthine network of tunnels finally opened out into a large, torch-lit cavern. Beads of brackish water trickled down its rough-hewn walls, sparkling in the feeble light, and a chilling vaporous mist hung suspended in the musty air.

Dale White lay on some kind of crude stone altar in the centre of the vault. But he now looked considerably different to the long-hauler who regularly passed through Dead End and always ate Philly cheesesteak and fries at Wanda's. Now he was little more than a powder-dry, shrivelled husk from which all the goodness had been extracted.

Surrounding the body was an equally odd group of men and women. There were about thirty of them. Not only did they all share the same red eyes as Wanda, right down to her distinctive thin-slit pupils, they also possessed overlarge canines — fangs.

Their mode of dress was strange, too. They looked as if they'd been plucked from the Old West. Here stood the man in the elegant grey frock coat and bed-of-flowers vest. There stood a group of three malnourished, whiskery miner-types in frayed band-collar work-shirts and brown pinstripe pants.

Sprinkled throughout the gathering were six gaunt-faced men wearing dark blue fatigue blouses and lighter blue wool pants along the outer seams of which ran thick yellow stripes. They, like the figure Ed had seen — or *thought* he'd seen — out in the desert, wore flat-crowned caps with black brims. George Steelgood was there too, for once without his wraparound sunglasses.

About a dozen women were scattered among the menfolk. Some were dressed in the faded crimson silks and satins of nineteenth-century soiled doves. Others wore long twill skirts, cotton blouses with high lace collars and leg o' mutton sleeves, sun bonnets and lace shawls.

The pale faces of each were hard and bony, their expressions tough, cold, almost brutal.

Perhaps most curious of all was a tall, squint-eyed man in a black sack coat and matching pants, who used the calloused palms of his bony hands to massage the butts of the two Colt revolvers he wore on the black leather cartridge belt around his narrow waist. This was Ethan Bayne, who had once, well over a century earlier, been a gunman and outlaw of some repute.

The blood-caked body seemed to exert a strange fascination over the assembly. The sight of what little blood remained at Dale's throat held them transfixed.

Until, that was, they heard the brisk, echoing clatter of footsteps coming closer from another tunnel, this one hacked out of the left-side wall.

Then, one by one, they dragged their gaze from the corpse, and the look of near-lust that the sight of blood had inspired was quickly replaced by fear.

The footsteps drew closer.

They were rhythmic, measured, militaristic.

A moment later Max Vickers appeared in the tunnel mouth, drew to a halt, stood with legs spread and white-knuckled fists on hips.

He was dressed in a long blue wool tunic upon the front of which sat two rows of shiny brass buttons. His matching pants were tucked into knee-high black boots, the waist of the jacket cinched tight by a polished black leather belt with a rectangular brass buckle upon which a spread eagle stood out in sharp relief.

An eight-foot snake whip, its tip filled with lead shot, was coiled in his right fist.

Perhaps it was just a trick of the flickering light, but now he looked harder, thinner and totally unforgiving. No smile, easy or otherwise, now touched his mouth, and his eyes no longer held even the pretence of warmth or welcome. They were flat and bead-like: dusky mirrors hiding a soul that was darker than dark.

At last he looked at the body. His gaze settled upon it for a full twenty seconds. Then he scanned the room.

'Who's responsible for this?' he demanded.

His voice echoed around the cold confines of the cavern.

No one spoke. Red eyes exchanged fearful glances. There was the uncomfortable shuffling of many feet.

'I repeat,' Max said. 'Who is responsible?'

Wanda, watching from the back of the

group with perhaps the greatest fear of all, was torn between owning up and staying quiet. She, like the others, had seen the colonel's wrath before and would never forget it. But what else could she have done? The hunger for blood had always been fiercer in her than it was in the others, and though it was hard for all of them, the others had always been able to control their urges. Hers, by contrast, would give her no peace until she satisfied them.

Even now she was still hungry.

Before she could decide what to do, one of the surly-looking men decked out in the ragged remains of a cavalry trooper's blue spat out a stream of tobacco juice and said hesitantly, 'Reckon we all are, Colonel.'

So fast that no-one even saw it, Max's right arm blurred back and then forward again, and the deceptively slim, sixteen-plait snake whip snapped through the air. An instant later the trooper — more accurately, deserter — yelped and staggered backwards, clutching the side of his head.

His neatly-severed right ear dropped to the ground at his feet.

The deserter himself fell to his knees, moaning. Max watched impassively as he snatched up the ear, blew dirt off it and then pressed it back to the side of his head.

Nothing happened immediately, but then the near-silence was broken by a faint sizzling sound as the ear reattached itself.

Though still in pain, the deserter heaved a sigh of relief.

Another man, this one middle-aged and dressed in black pants and a crimson vest over a white shirt, stepped forward. He had fair curly hair, long, slightly darker sideburns and a heavy steer-horn moustache. 'Colonel,' he said in a deep baritone, 'we never meant to kill him. But it's been days since we tasted blood, an' I guess . . . well, we figured we deserved — '

Even as he spoke, Max threw the whip aside and underwent an almost instant transformation. The fleshy tone of his skin lightened; his face appeared to ooze and ripple and grow more ridged with bone;

his eyes sank far back into his head and turned the same unholy red as those of his companions.

A second later he grabbed the speaker by his hair and yanked his head back to expose his pale, pulsing throat. With one deep, snarling bite, he tore the man's jugular out.

Everyone gasped.

The man hung as if weightless in Max's grasp, head tilted back, shocked eyes staring sightlessly toward the cavern's high, shadowed ceiling, his throat a bloody mess from which hung stringy crimson threads of flesh.

A moment later Max tossed the body aside. As it hit the cavern floor it vanished in a short-lived burst of white-hot flame.

The others took a horrified step backwards and a fearful mutter ran through them, for this was a fate they all dreaded.

Max glared at his audience, blood staining his fangs which, in the unnatural light, appeared to be the colour of silver.

'You all know why I saved you from the cholera,' he said, enraged. 'As humans you were the worst of the worst. Everybody in Silverton despised you, and with good reason. You were whores and cheats, road-agents and philanderers, killers, abortionists, bigamists, swindlers and mealy-mouthed deserters, cowards, the scum of the earth!'

'I alone welcomed your wickedness, your depravity, and this — ' he gestured to what was left of Dale White, ' — this is how you repay me?'

The man in the grey frock coat and bed-of-flowers vest said quietly, 'Colonel, we're sorry — '

'Sorry?' hissed Max. 'You *fools!* Don't you *get* it? This man was an outsider! He may have a family or friends or even an employer who'll report his disappearance. Next thing you know, everyone's looking for him — the police, the F.B.I . . . perhaps even the Seekers.'

This last word sent another fearful reaction through the gathering. Max was glad to see it, for if they should be scared of anything in this world or the next, it was the Seekers.

'We're safe here,' he continued. 'And as

long as we don't draw attention to ourselves by *killing* anyone, the townsfolk will never even suspect our true nature. Remember, we *need* them. Not only do they provide us with an endless supply of food, but with each bite we increase our numbers and grow stronger.'

He looked at them. No one dared to meet his gaze and that pleased him, too.

'For centuries our kind has ruled the night. But now organisations like the Seekers have taken it upon themselves to exterminate us . . . and as we all know, they're winning the war. We must tread carefully, watch our every move, show patience and restraint, bide our time, grow strong and multiply until . . . '

He deliberately let the word hang heavily in the dank air, knowing that he had them now, that they were once again his to command.

At last he added, ' . . . until we can finally reveal ourselves and fight back in the sure and certain knowledge that we simply cannot *lose*.'

⋆　⋆　⋆

After Ed paid the check, they drove out of town in Fiona's green Chevy Tahoe until they came to a ridge that overlooked the desert. They sat there for a while, just looking out at the rise and fall of the distant mountains, showing black against the deep, star-scattered purple of the night sky, and listening to the yip-yipping of prowling coyotes.

'Man, it's so beautiful out here,' Ed said. 'I've spent so much time in the city that I'd forgotten how bright the stars really are.' Hearing himself, he suddenly threw her a self-conscious grin. 'Maybe you should tell the Chamber of Commerce. A postcard of this would do for Dead End what oranges once did for California.'

Fiona didn't reply immediately. When at last she did, it was to say softly, 'You talk too much.'

He turned to face her. 'So shut me up.'

She did.

She leaned forward and kissed him gently on the lips, and he responded in kind, gently at first but with rapidly-increasing desire.

They held each other then, held each other close and kissed harder, each exploring the other, and because Ed had his eyes tight shut, he didn't see the faint crimson wash that suddenly entered hers.

He alternately kissed and nibbled his way across her jaw and down along her neck, and as he did so the red glow in her eyes grew deeper and more intense. A small, soft groan escaped her lips as they peeled back to reveal long white fangs, glistening in the light of the full moon.

She didn't want to do this, she really *didn't* . . . but oh, by all that was unholy she really *did*, too, and the pull of him, his warmth, the powerful throb of blood coursing through his veins was too much to resist . . .

Almost.

She came very, very close to biting him. But would never know for sure whether or not she'd have actually gone through with it, because he chose that moment to pull back from her and catch his breath, and she quickly turned her head away from him so that he wouldn't see the change that had come upon her.

He sensed that something was wrong, though. She seemed tense now, stiff and suddenly uncommunicative. Frowning, he said, 'Are you okay?' And then, with surprise, 'You're trembling . . . '

'It . . . it's getting chilly,' she managed after a moment, her voice deep, choked, weirdly formal. 'We'd better start back.'

Puzzled, he said, 'Did I do something wrong? If I offended you — '

'You didn't,' she said, and finally looked at him — through normal, brown eyes.

'Then I don't get it. Why are you shutting me out like this?'

'I'm not.'

'The hell you're not.'

'Well,' she said, trying to control her mixed emotions, 'you'll just have to take it whichever way you like.'

He stared at her a moment longer, then shook his head. 'I guess I will,' he said finally. 'But that doesn't mean I have to like it.'

6

She dropped him outside the hotel. When he went to kiss her goodnight she turned her face away from him and he felt a sudden stab of anger, because he liked her and he'd thought she liked him too, and he wanted to know what he'd done to change that.

She released the brake, said a barely-audible goodnight and drove away. But as she reached the corner her eyes suddenly sharpened on something far ahead of her, and she stiffened visibly. A moment later she nodded and whispered dully, as if in a trance, 'Yes, father. I'm coming . . . '

★   ★   ★

Sitting cross-legged on the hotel's flat roof, Jake Simms frowned at the screen of the small, hand-held computer he'd been studying. With the stylus in his free hand he tapped at the miniature keyboard for a few moments. The screen flashed briefly. Then Jake ran his near-black eyes across it again and smiled in cool approval.

Everything was looking good.

* * *

Fiona drove out toward the old silver mines. The night seemed darker now, as if something had blacked out the stars and even forced the moon to withdraw into itself. Only her headlights showed her the road ahead. It was empty.

At last something inside her, some unheard command, made her slow to a stop at the side of the road. She switched off the engine and silence settled back across the wilderness.

Without warning, the headlights went out.

And a fraction of a second later —

Max appeared out of nowhere right beside the car, tore open the door and ripped her from her seat.

She went flying across the blacktop, rolled and came up unsteadily on her hands and knees, her black-streaked-with-red hair awry.

Still in uniform, his coiled snake-whip hanging from his belt, Max stalked toward her, his brisk, even footfalls clicking through the silence of the night. His head had sunken into his shoulders and his hands were twisted into claws.

He came to a halt above her, then reached down with lightning rapidity and grabbed her around the throat.

'How dare you disobey me!'

Instinctively she grabbed his wrist and tried to make him let her go. But he was too strong, stronger than anyone could ever possibly imagine.

He picked her up and held her at arm's-length. Her feet dangling off the ground, she kicked desperately. A moment later he flung her from him. She crashed into the brush beside the road, moaned and again slowly, doggedly rose to her hands and knees.

'P-Please, father,' she whispered.

He stood above her, his mouth stretching wide in a snarl that revealed his silver-looking fangs.

'*Please*,' she sobbed. 'I beg you . . . spare me.'

Something, some odd, unexpectedly plaintive quality in her voice seemed to touch him, and almost reluctantly he surrendered some of his rage. His clawed hands flexed and relaxed, flexed and relaxed, and gradually the tightness in his face eased.

'I should destroy you,' he rasped. 'I should destroy you as I would destroy any other vampire who dared to disobey me. How else is a man to rule others when even his own *daughter* defies him?'

She knelt before him, her head down, trembling.

'Speak up!' he roared. 'Have you nothing to say in your defence?'

She muttered something.

'What was that?'

'Nothing that would excuse my behaviour,' she repeated.

He looked up at the vast expanse of the sky and shook his head. 'For decades I've trained you to ignore your human emotions.'

'Father, it's not your fault. You've done

'everything you could.'

'But clearly I haven't done enough. Otherwise you would have sought my permission before trying to bite him.'

She sobbed softly.

He turned away from her, brushed imaginary dust from his tunic's distinctive shoulder boards, each one black with a lemon yellow border and two embroidered silver oak leaves.

'What's so special about him that made you betray me?' he demanded.

'I don't know. I only know that before today I've never felt like this about any human being.' Her gaze fixed on his back then quickly, guiltily shuttled away again. 'Not even my mother.'

At the mention of his dead wife, the tension in Max's shoulders ebbed noticeably. 'I was so proud of you when she died,' he said, turning to her. 'Not one tear did you shed.'

Sensing an opening, she said eagerly, 'If you let me live, father, I'll make you proud of me again. I swear.'

He looked down at her, weighing his reply. Finally he whispered, 'You had *better*.'

In his hotel room, Ed lay on the bed and turned Fiona's business card thoughtfully between his fingers. He still didn't understand what had happened to sour their evening, but maybe tomorrow he'd go see her again and try to clear up whatever misunderstanding might have developed between them.

He closed his eyes, suddenly tired. His head had started aching again and he guessed the after-effects of the crash were finally catching up with him. He sat up and began to punch his pillows into shape — when there was a knock at the door.

He got up and went to the door, hoping that Fiona had had second thoughts and come back to apologise —

But when he opened the door, no one there.

He frowned and looked down.

At his feet lay a box that had been turned upside-down, so that it covered something on the floor.

Suspiciously, he looked up and down the hallway. It was empty. Cautiously he toed the box over onto its side and thought, *I'll be damned*.

The box had concealed a cool-looking black felt hat, just like the ones old-time US Cavalry officers used to wear, but with one exception — the addition of a wolf-skin hat-band.

He picked up the hat and the box and turned back into his room, heeling the door shut behind him. He threw the box onto a chair, put the hat on — taking care to settle it gently over the cut on his forehead — and checked himself in the mirror. It was a perfect fit.

He posed for a moment, squinting *à la* Robert Mitchum, then squared his shoulders and saluted himself. Just then there was another knock.

When he opened the door another surprise awaited him.

Wanda was standing in the hallway, wearing a short, sexy red and black satin dress. She looked good enough to eat. Without a word she raised the pint bottle of Jim Beam she held in her left hand and gave it a little jiggle.

'Surprise!' She pushed past him into

the room. 'I hope you like bourbon.'

Before he could reply, she disappeared into the bathroom.

'W-What are you doing here?' he asked, not moving.

She reappeared almost immediately, only this time she was stark naked.

'Next question,' she said.

Ed nudged his new hat back and shook his head. In the soft yellow light of the bedside lamp she looked like a fantasy come to life. Her figure was perfectly proportioned, with good, strong shoulders, medium-sized breasts, a trim waist, flared hips, slender legs.

She handed him one of two glasses she'd found in the bathroom, took the door from his grasp, closed it softly and slipped on the chain. Then she brushed past him, sat on the bed and raised her own glass in toast. 'Cheers.'

'Look,' he began awkwardly, not sure how to handle this, 'don't think I'm not flattered, but — .'

She pouted. 'Ah shit, you're not a gay cowboy, are you?'

'Not the last time I checked.'

'Then get your butt over here and we'll discuss world economics,' she said with another bubbly giggle. 'Or we could just get bombed and fuck our brains out. You choose.'

He came over and stood before her, still not really knowing what to do or say without offending her.

'Unless of course I'm not your type . . . ?'

As she spoke, she reached for the front of his pants and her eyebrows went up. 'Oooh. No need to answer *that* question.'

Rising, she put her arms around his neck and tried to draw him towards her. But still he refused to cooperate.

'What's with you?' she asked petulantly. 'We both know you want me.'

'Maybe I prefer to make all the running.'

She shrugged, settled back on the mattress and slowly spread her legs. 'Well, then,' she purred, 'start running.'

Although it wasn't easy, he stood his ground, his heart thudding. Making a feeble stab at diplomacy he suggested, 'How about a raincheck?'

She looked as if she'd been slapped. 'Are you *serious?*'

His silence was answer enough.

'Well, suit yourself, honey.' Getting up, she padded back into the bathroom. While she was gone, he took a hasty gulp of his drink, hoping it might steady him. It didn't.

When she reappeared she was dressed again and seemed to have calmed down. As she walked toward him, she offered a philosophical little smile and raised her glass.

'Here's to no hard feelin's, then,' she said — and threw the contents of the glass in his face.

He staggered backwards, temporarily blinded by the bourbon, pawing at his stinging eyes. Instantly she was on him like a tiger. She kneed him in the groin and he doubled over with a grunt. While he was down she kneed him in the face, sending him sprawling, his hat rolling into a corner.

She crossed the room in a series of fast, fluid steps, and with every one her face changed: her skin bleached and tightened across her skull; her eyes dropped back in their sockets and reddened; the pupils shrank and stretched until they were no more than slits; and as she opened her mouth her canines seemed to grow, extending slowly but smoothly, to long, needle-sharp points.

In that moment Ed realised where he'd seen her before; the red and black satin dress, the blonde hair with the single white streak sweeping back from the left temple; she'd been in his dream; the saloon girl the young soldier had been about to shoot in the face —

She rushed him again. With no option he powered up and went to meet her, determined to deck her with a round-house right and then call for help.

He let go a beauty of a punch that caught her right on the chin. But though it rocked her and sent her staggering back, it didn't put her down. In fact, if the searing pain Ed felt shooting up his arm was anything to go by, it probably hurt him more than it hurt her.

Regaining her balance Wanda sneered at him, reminding him of an angry cobra that needs no special reason to strike.

She came at him again and he moved quickly to put the bed between them. His face was smarting, his eyes watering, and his groin felt like it was on fire.

She leapt onto and over the bed, arms outstretched, fingers like talons questing for his throat. The bedside lamp splashed her shadow long and distorted across the ceiling, like spilled ink.

Before he could avoid her, she rammed into him and they went down onto the floor with Wanda, now straddling him, trying to strangle him.

He tried to twist away, hoping to dislodge her, but she was too powerful for him. Her fingers dug into the flesh of his throat. He grabbed her wrists and frantically did his best to pull them loose.

When that didn't work, he twisted one final time and finally succeeded in toppling her. With a scream of rage she rolled one way and he rolled the other.

She came up to her knees but he was faster. On his feet now and trying to ignore the pain of his injuries, he aimed a kick at her face. But she caught his foot, twisted and hurled him away from her. He crashed into the cheap wardrobe, bounced off it and collapsed on the floor.

She was on him instantly, hissing now, her tongue flicking forth from between her lips like that of the angry snake she so resembled.

Grabbing him, she picked him up and held him aloft as if he weighed less than a feather, then opened her mouth to bite him. As she drew him slowly, inexorably toward her, her eyes shone like ice-cold fire.

Desperately he croaked, '*O Salutaris Hostia, Quae coeli pandas ostium. Bella premunt hostilia; Da robur, fer auxilium.*'

Her eyes widened, and as alien as they were, he could still see emotion within them: surprise, rage, pain.

'*Uni trinoque Domino,*' he continued, grinding the ancient prayer of protection from between clenched teeth, '*Sit sempiterna gloria: Qui vitam sine termino, Nobis donet in patria!*'

She gave a scream of rage and tossed him away from her. Once again he slammed hard against the wardrobe, this time splintering one of its doors.

He slumped to the floor, wondering what the fuck was going on. He reached deep inside himself, his determination to defeat her galvanising him so that he clawed his way back to his feet even as Wanda rushed him again, still screaming with rage.

She ducked under his arms, came around behind him and threw herself onto his back, trying to sink her fangs into his throat. Staggered, Ed reached back, grabbed her and threw her over his head.

She slammed to the floor, rolled and came up snarling. He kicked her in the face. She fell back, slamming into the wall. Wind knocked out of her, she paused for a moment to catch her breath — and before she could launch another assault, four men came up behind Ed and grabbed her by the arms.

Startled, Ed realised it was the rockers, the *Platinum Dead*.

'Whoa there, lady!' yelled Jake Simms.

Ed wearily stumbled back, panting.

Beau brushed aside his long black,

green and orange hair and grinned at Ed. 'Hey, man, we don't wanna jam up your sex life, but can you at keep the noise down? We're trying to *compose* here!'

Struggling in their grip, Wanda angrily bared her fangs and hissed at him.

The other rockers grinned appreciatively. 'Say, baby, who's your dentist?' Kyle kidded her. The rest of the band cracked up.

Ed, seeing that Beau and Jake were about to let her go, yelled, 'No! Don't! She — '

But he was too late.

Wanda jerked away from them, ran across the room and hurled herself out the window.

Momentarily, Ed and the rockers could only stand in shock as she crashed through glass and frame and vanished into the dark night. Then Ed ran to what was left of the window, the *Platinum Dead* close on his heels.

They expected to see Wanda splattered on the sidewalk. Instead they were just in time to see her execute a graceful somersault in mid-air and land lightly on her feet.

Giving Ed a hateful look, she raced off down the street.

Jake grinned. 'Cool!'

Brad agreed. 'Man, that is one tough chick.'

Ed glanced from one to the other. He was shaking, but the band acted as if they encountered this kind of thing every day of the week.

'Come on, pilgrims,' Jake said, heading for the door. 'Back to work.' He winked at Ed and pointed his forefinger at him as if it were a gun barrel. 'Stay cool, dude.'

'Wait up,' Ed said. 'How did you guys get in here?'

'Walked through the wall,' Jake said. 'How else?'

He grinned and hummed the opening bars of the *Twilight Zone* theme. The other rockers joined in. When they got to the door, however, Jake pointed to the chain that was hanging loose and said, 'Maybe you should use this in future?'

As Ed closed the door behind them, he looked at the chain. He could have sworn Wanda had latched it.

Once he'd recovered, he went downstairs and told the duty clerk that there had been an accident with his window. The clerk, a bespectacled forty year-old with a long neck and a bobbing Adam's apple, gave him a strange look, went outside and inspected the sidewalk. When he returned he said, 'Are you sure, Mr Knight? Everything looks all right from the outside.'

'What're you talking about? The window's shattered. The sidewalk must be covered in glass.'

'It's not.'

'Well, the window's broken, all right. Come up and look for yourself, if you don't believe me.'

'I've already looked from outside,' said the duty clerk. 'It's fine.'

Too tired to argue, Ed went back upstairs. When he let himself into his room, he saw that the duty clerk was right. The window was unbroken and closed tight against the chilling, wind-blown darkness.

Unable to explain to himself what exactly was going on, he stored the night's eerie events away and cleared up the rest of the room. As he retrieved his hat and brushed it off, he wondered if there were any others in town like Wanda? And if there were, was Fiona one of them?

He had no idea. But he was damn' sure going to find out.

7

Early the following morning he showered, dressed, grabbed his new hat and made directly for Wanda's Café. The place was busy with the breakfast trade, but there was no sign of Wanda.

Instead, he found Fiona working behind the counter.

As he sat on a stool, she bustled past carrying two plates of hotcakes. She was dressed casually in jeans and a t-shirt, her face flushed, her hair a little straggly. Seeing him, she said almost mechanically, 'Be right with you.'

She came back a short time later and poured him a cup of coffee. 'Before you ask,' she said, taking great care not to look at him, 'I'm filling in for Wanda. Her mom got sick and she had to go to Tucson to help out.'

'She tell you this in person?' he asked casually.

'No. She called me. Why?'

'How long will she be gone?'

'She didn't say. But I've already lined up someone to fill in for her.' At last she looked him in the face, reacting when she saw the bruises Wanda had given him the previous night. 'My God, what happened to you?'

'Do you want the long or the short version?'

Before she could reply, a stocky man in his early sixties joined them and held out his check to Fiona. 'Hey, Doc. Wanna take my money?'

Ed looked him over. A fine-looking man in his day, he now had a jowly face, baggy blue eyes and an unclipped walrus moustache the same pure white as the hair that was just visible beneath his curl-brimmed black Stetson. He wore an ash-grey suit cut western-style and a horse's-head bolo tie at the buttoned collar of his lightweight white shirt. He looked tanned and comfortably off, and as he gave Ed an easy smile he revealed slightly crooked teeth that were just beginning to yellow.

'How was breakfast, Hal?' Fiona said,

moving behind the register.

Great as always. Wanda sick?' he added.

'Uh-uh. Just taking a few days off.' She rang up the check and gave him his change.

Hal smiled congenially at Ed. 'New in town, mister?'

'Just got in yesterday.'

'You'll like it here. Dead End's a nice town.'

'So everyone keeps telling me.'

'They're just trying to make you feel at home. What happened to your head, if I may ask?' he asked.

Ed swapped glances with Fiona then said: 'I tripped.'

'Looks like your handiwork,' Hal said to Fiona.

'Guilty as charged.'

'I meant that as a compliment,' Hal said, laughing. Then to Ed: 'Doc here is one of the reasons this is such a great place to live.'

'Makes sense,' Ed said.

'Will you two stop,' Fiona said. 'You're embarrassing me.'

'Wouldn't want to do that,' Hal said.

He clapped Ed on the shoulder. 'I hope you stick around, son. Then you'll see why we're all so proud of this town. It's small and doesn't offer some of the big city amenities, but trust me: it has a habit of growing on people.' He left, the bell above the door tinkling behind him.

'Chamber of Commerce?' Ed said, wincing as he sipped his coffee and it stung his split lips.

'Close,' Fiona said. 'He's our Mayor.'

'I pegged him as your local snake-oil salesman.'

'Actually he's a *used* car salesman.'

'Even better.'

'Oh, Hal Blaylock's not so bad. Being Mayor is a voluntary job but he really tries his best to make Dead End a decent place to live.' She saw more customers entering and grabbed some menus. 'That version you were going to give me — better make it the short one.'

He said, straight-faced: 'I was attacked by a horny vampire.'

He expected her to burst out laughing. Instead she said: 'Sorry I asked.'

'I'm serious,' Ed said. And then, before

he could stop himself, 'I'm serious about a *lot* of things, Fiona.'

'I'm sorry,' she said, indicating all the customers who were waiting to order, 'but this really isn't a good time.'

'I know. But I need to explain about last night. I was wrong to expect you to — '

'You weren't wrong,' she interrupted, putting her hand over his. 'But can we talk about this later?'

'Sure. When?'

A thought hit her. 'What have you got planned for today?'

'Nothing,' he lied.

'Then come with me while I make my house-calls.'

'Our second date. How romantic.'

'Actually, I think you'll enjoy meeting my patients. They live out near the mines, and it'll give us a chance to talk on the way.'

It was that last part that sold him. 'Okay. Will you call me?'

She nodded, more relieved than pleased, then said: 'By the way. I like your hat — Cowboy.'

Closing the café door behind him, Hal Blaylock walked to the curb where his navy blue Chevy Suburban was parked. As usual, he had a busy day ahead of him. In addition to his day job there were building permits to consider, an overdue water and wastewater report to wade through, reports on capital improvements and fiscal budgets to study before the next council meeting and the formation of a new community services department to oversee.

Public service, as he so often reminded himself, was a harsh taskmaster.

But when a silver Ford pickup drove past, bearing the legend *CATLIN CON-STRUCTION*, followed by a crescent-shaped *C* with a four-pointed star between the two curved tips, he paused and thoughtfully scratched his chin. Then, climbing into the Chevy, he gunned the engine and cruised after the truck.

★   ★   ★

Sam Cocheta was topping off the oil in his tractor when the Catlin Construction truck went by. A few seconds later the Mayor drove past. Seeing Sam, he honked and waved.

Sam waved back and watched Blaylock's Suburban turn left, onto the same side street the construction truck had taken. The Apache's weathered face was unreadable. After a moment, however, he set the oil can down and lowered himself slowly to a crouch.

He closed his eyes, mentally preparing himself for what would follow, and then began to draw a series of deliberate streaks and shapes in the sand. When he was finished, he opened his eyes again and stared at his handiwork.

His expression hardened.

He'd drawn a crescent moon with a four-pointed star hanging between its two curved tips.

*   *   *

The truck was parked outside the front office of an old motel that looked just about ready for the wrecking ball. A gaudy sign beside the entrance read:

SUNRISE MOTOR HOTEL
TV — PHONE — SWIMMING
POOL — COFFEE SHOP
COOLED BY REFRIDGERATION
VACANCIES

Beneath it, a second, newer sign added:

FUTURE HOME
OF
CATLIN CONSTRUCTION

The empty, weed-choked parking lot was hemmed in on three sides by short, run-down rows of fading, single-storey adobe apartments with Mexican-style red-tiled roofs. The apartments had once been painted coral pink, but over the years the paint had peeled and flaked, so that now the place reeked of neglect and squalor.

Hal Blaylock drove into the parking lot and killed the engine. Getting out, he pulled his Stetson squarely atop his head, gave his lapels a quick, business-like tug and entered the front office.

The place had long-since been stripped of everything of value. What was left was covered in dust. A few recent handprints showed on the front desk, but aside from these the place looked and smelled as if it had been empty forever.

Two men in jeans and hard hats were examining blueprints in the small room behind the desk. When Blaylock cleared his throat to get their attention, one of them quickly rolled the plans up while the other came out to meet him.

'Mornin', fellers,' Blaylock said cheerfully. 'Mind if I ask what you're up to?'

The other man, tall, muscular, about forty-five, said mildly, 'And you are . . . ?'

'Hal Blaylock, Mayor.'

The man relaxed. He had close-set grey eyes and yellow-brown stubble. 'I'm Pete Johnson, foreman. That there's my associate, Roy Drake.'

'Well, let me be the first to welcome you to Dead End,' said Blaylock as they shook hands. 'Believe me, the town council was thrilled when Catlin Construction announced that it was settling here.'

'My boss'll be happy to hear that,' Johnson said. 'We were planning to stop by your office later today, just to let you know we'll be tearing this place down tomorrow.'

Blaylock glanced sourly around. 'Sooner the better.'

'It is pretty grim,' Johnson agreed. An awkward silence followed his comment, until he broke it with a businesslike, 'Anyway, if it's okay with you, Mayor, we'll get back to work. Got a lot to do and very little time to do it in.'

'Sure, sure. See you boys later.'

Blaylock touched the brim of his hat, turned and left.

Johnson and Drake exchanged relieved looks. Drake then unrolled the blueprints again and they continued studying the plans.

They depicted a tall, pyramid-shaped structure crowned by a four-pointed, star-shaped antenna. Below it were two words:

STAR TOWER

Down at the local Wal-Mart, a young woman stood on tiptoe and reached for a box of *Cinnamon Chex* that remained stubbornly just beyond her grasp.

'Here,' said a soft voice behind her. 'Let me get that for you, ma'am.'

She turned, startled, in time to see the Settler in the grey frock coat and bed-of-flowers vest take down the box she'd been after.

'Why, thank you,' she said as he dropped it into her cart.

He doffed his coachman's hat and bowed gallantly. He was slim and pale, somewhere in his early thirties, with a long, well-defined but seriously under-nourished face. He wore his blue-black hair short and oiled: she noticed that it curled appealingly at his nape.

'I've often seen you around town, ma'am, but I don't believe we've ever been formally introduced.' He had a quiet, cultured voice with a gentle Southern accent. 'My name is Dolan, ma'am. Quincy Dolan.'

The girl's long corn-bright hair framed a plain, freckled face with blue eyes and sad lips. She wasn't used to such old-world charm and it made her blush. Single mothers in their early twenties didn't encounter that kind of thing too often, especially in the welfare line. In fact, male attention, charming or otherwise, had become something of a rarity ever since her husband had walked out on her and the baby seven months earlier, so she was flattered by the tall man's interest.

'I'm Cathy,' she said self-consciously. 'Cathy Maynard.'

'I'm honoured to make your acquaintance at long last,' he said pleasantly.

Behind his wraparound glasses, however, Dolan's eyes were unreadable.

★   ★   ★

As soon as the tour bus pulled up outside the hotel, Jake and the rest of the band emerged, dressed as always as if it were the dead of winter. Gerry Irwin watched them climb aboard and head for the back of the bus, there to breakfast on Barq's root beer, sugar cookies and cheez doodles until they reached their destination.

Only Jake bothered to acknowledge him and that was because he wanted to make sure Gerry understood where he had to take them. Gerry took the directions Jake had written out for him, scanned them briefly and put them on the dash. He then gunned the engine and pointed the bus toward Main.

As they reached the intersection Jake's attention was taken by a sudden flurry of car-horns, and he came back to take a look at what was going on through the windshield. A green Chevy Tahoe had stalled in the middle of Main, and impatient drivers, none of whom were prepared to give way to each other, were trying to weave around it.

'Stop the bus,' he said.

There was a break in the long line of traffic and Gerry was just about to make the turn. 'What?'

'Stop the freakin' bus.'

Gerry threw him a murderous look but

bit his tongue and thought acidly, *Okay. You're the freakin' boss.*

Jake hopped down and dodged the crawling traffic to reach the stalled Chevy. He wasn't so much interested in playing Good Samaritan as he was in getting to meet the vehicle's darkly attractive driver. 'Run out of gas?' he called as he covered the last couple of yards.

Fiona looked out at him and shook her head. 'I don't know. It just died on me.'

'Could be you flooded the carb,' he said. 'Here, let me give it a whirl.'

Without waiting for a reply he opened the door and squeezed inside, giving her no option but to slide over into the passenger seat. He studied the controls for a moment, then floored the gas pedal. 'Sometimes, if you keep the gas pedal all the way down . . . '

He turned on the ignition. The engine struggled for a moment, then finally started.

'*Voilà*,' he said.

She heaved a sigh of relief. 'Thanks. Or should that be *merçi*? Either way, you're a life-saver.' Impulsively she extended her right hand. 'Fiona Vickers.'

Taking her hand, he slipped his sunglasses down a notch so that he could look her right in the eye. He had very nice eyes, she thought: black and mysterious.

'Jake Simms,' he said, and dazzled her with a killer smile.

'You're with the, uh . . . band, right?' she said.

'They're with *me*,' he corrected.

'Well, th-thanks for your help . . . Jake.'

'Any time, babe. Maybe I'll see you around?'

She nodded. 'Maybe you will.'

At last he allowed her to take her hand back. But just before he closed the door behind him, he gave a parting grin the Devil himself would have been proud of.

★　★　★

Hal Blaylock was hard at work when his phone buzzed. Still poring over paperwork, he lifted the receiver and said distractedly, 'What is it, Sharon?'

'There's a Mr Knight here to see you, Mayor,' said his secretary.

The name made Blaylock sit up straight. 'Send him right in.'

A moment later the door opened and Ed walked in. Blaylock was already on his feet and waiting expectantly behind his desk, right hand thrust forward.

Ed closed the door softly behind him and they shook.

'We meet again,' said Blaylock. 'Thanks for coming, Mr Knight.'

'Call me Ed.'

Blaylock nodded. 'I know how busy the Seekers are.'

'From what you told me on the phone,' Ed said, 'and what I experienced first-hand last night, how could we refuse? You've got quite a problem here, Mayor. In fact I might almost say you've got a hell of a problem.'

★   ★   ★

According to Jake, it was called the Place of White Pebbles. To Gerry Irwin, sitting in the shade thrown by the tour bus and fanning himself with his baseball cap, it looked just like any other part of this

Godforsaken shit-hole.

Everywhere he looked scarred amber boulders stood side by side or leaned crookedly against each other. Wasps and flies buzzed around the red stems of dogbane and the white trumpets of jimson weed.

Studying his bleak surroundings, Gerry shook his head. He'd just completed what must have been his weirdest task for the band yet: stringing power cables from the bus to the crude, roughly oval amphitheatre nestled between the boulders thirty yards away.

Here the band had painstakingly collected up almost all the white pebbles with which this stretch of desert seemed to be littered and placed them side by side in order to create some kind of picture or symbol in the hot sand.

Gerry hadn't been able to make out what it was at first. He'd been too busy rolling out cables and rigging up connections, setting out guitars and amplifiers and fixing up Jake's Roland Fantom G-8 synthesizer because, according to Jake, this was 'the ideal place to jam.'

It was only once he'd finished and was

climbing back through a gap in the rocks that put him at a slightly higher elevation that he bothered to look down at their creation.

It was a four-pointed star sitting between the tips of a large crescent, which had also been fashioned from white pebbles. And next to that was an upside-down crescent with spike-shaped rays emanating from it.

Man, he thought as he headed back to the shade of the tour bus. *These fucks are getting crazier by the day.*

* * *

After he left the Mayor's office Ed stopped by *Wanda's*, saw that Wanda's temporary replacement had finally taken over and then headed for Fiona's office. To his surprise, she was already waiting for him outside, in her SUV.

'My, you're keen,' he said as he climbed in beside her.

She shrugged. 'I just have a feeling that this is going to be . . . enlightening . . . for you.'

He frowned. She seemed jumpy and trying not to let it show, but maybe it was just his imagination. 'Then let's go,' he said.

She drove them out of town and into the desert, heading for the dirt road that led to the old silver mines.

'Heard from Wanda?' he asked.

She kept her eyes on the road ahead. 'No. But I didn't expect to. Not while she's taking care of her mother.'

'No, I guess not.'

'Is anything wrong? Did you want to talk to her about something?'

'Nothing important.'

'Good. Because I'd like you to keep your mind on us.'

'Us?' He couldn't keep the surprise from his voice. 'After last night, I didn't think — '

' — I wanted to be with you?' she finished. 'Nothing could be further from the truth.'

'Well, you sure have a funny way of showing it.'

'I know, and I'm sorry for acting the way I did. I guess I got . . . scared. I've never felt those kinds of emotions before. Besides, I'd just met you and — '

' — you didn't see much future in falling for a drifter, right? A drifter who might even yet turn into a frog.'

'Please,' she said. 'Don't joke. I'm serious.'

He realised then that she was in fact deadly serious, and it went some of the way towards explaining why she seemed so edgy.

He was just about to assure her that he was equally serious about this when his cell phone buzzed. He dug it out, checked the caller ID and winced. 'Sorry. I have to take this.' He put the phone to his ear, listened a moment, then said, 'Okay.'

He ended the call and said, 'I have to go back.'

'What?'

'I'm sorry.'

'Well . . . can't it wait?'

'Uh-huh. Look, just let me off here. We're not that far from town. I can walk back.'

Fiona faced front again so that he wouldn't notice the frustrated red glimmer that began to creep into her eyes.

She'd promised to deliver him to her father. It was to be her way of proving herself to him. And she still could, if she chose to take Ed to the mine by force . . . couldn't she?

It should all be so easy, just to take by force or guile whatever you wanted and not spare a single thought for your victim. But for Fiona it had always been anything but easy.

Not for the first time she cursed her emotions, the moods and feelings that would always separate her from her father and his kind. Her mother had often told her that humanity was a wonderful gift, but it was also a heavy load to bear when your father despised everything that was human.

But there might still a way to do this without resorting to brute force. Somehow she managed a smile and slowed down. 'Don't be silly,' she said. 'It's over a hundred out there. You'd fry.'

'I've got my hat, remember.'

'Oh, sure. That's going to be a *big* help.'

Without another word she turned the

SUV around and started back toward town. 'Listen, there's a dance tonight at the Clubhouse. You know that band, the *Platinum Dead?*'

'We've met.'

'My dad's arranged for them to play for us. Do you think you can tear yourself away from whatever else concerns you to show up?'

'I could be persuaded — on one condition.'

'Name it.'

'You save the first dance for me.'

She smiled. 'It starts at eight.'

'I'll be there.'

★ ★ ★

As the afternoon wore on and the sun slowly dipped behind the western hills, the vampires began to stir in their dark, subterranean cavern. Curled up behind rocks in pairs or hanging singly from pockmarked walls and vaulted ceiling, they gradually began to twitch, then flex, then stretch and finally surface from the deep, dreamless sleep of the dead.

Ethan Bayne was first to awake. He was always the first to awake. He'd spent most of his adult life sleeping light and living with one eye on his shoulder. It didn't matter the reason: lawmen, bounty men or just men who wanted to make a name for themselves by beating him to the draw; after a while it had gotten so that Bayne slept light.

Even in *death* he slept light.

A tall, spare man with a dark, horseshoe moustache and pale, hollow cheeks that had been pitted by some childhood illness, he'd lived a hard life but a good one, inasmuch as it had been to his taste. The ability to instil fear and adulation in others had been like a drug to him, and just like a drug, it had been addictive.

Until he'd learned to handle his two Navy .36s, he'd been lost in the crowd, just one among many. But his exceptional skill with those heavy, long-barrelled Colts had eventually raised him head and shoulders above the rest, and that was just where he wanted to be.

His guns, and still more his willingness

to use them at the slightest provocation, gave him power and brought him grudging respect. They made other men quake or crave only to walk in his shadow.

So yes, it had been a good life. And when the colonel had offered him the chance to live it without end, he'd jumped at it.

But over the years he'd come to realise that immortality was a double-edged sword. For where was the point in living forever, of enjoying such physical power that sometimes it was all a man could do just to keep it contained, if that life meant you couldn't live outdoors for any length of time or breathe good, clean air or feel the wind on your face and a strong horse keeping you one jump ahead of a posse?

Immortality . . .

In order to have this life he'd sacrificed whatever dark, corrupted thing had passed for his soul. But instead of enjoying it, he'd ended up enduring it.

There were no more banks to rob or mail-coaches to stop, no more challengers to face down, no more posses to dodge. Instead there was only this living death that was neither living nor death; of being tucked away below ground and told to curb what had become a natural instinct to hunt and kill and drink fresh, hot blood.

Bayne watched his companions stir. They were a miserable bunch to spend eternity with. He despised them as he despised the colonel and the thing that the colonel had made of him, a thing that was at once incredibly powerful and yet almost completely, pitifully power*less*.

As he stood up and brushed himself off, he noticed that one of the deserters, a Pole called Ivan Gorski, was staring at him from the other side of the cavern.

When Bayne's narrow blue eyes settled on him, Gorski, on his knees, slowly turned his attention back to the card game he and his fellow deserters were setting up to pass what remained of the day.

Damn that miserable Pole! They'd never gotten along. And though Bayne would never admit it, he had come to hate Gorski for one very simple reason: that he'd never shown Bayne the respect and reverence he figured he deserved.

Whenever the other men clustered around Bayne and asked him to regale them with stories of life on the owl hoot trail, Gorski always snorted and shook his big head and lumbered away. If ever one of the women expressed an interest in Bayne, Gorski immediately laid claim to her, or taught her not to go near Bayne again by blacking an eye or breaking a rib.

Gorski . . . He never backed down, never stepped aside, never made way.

Which meant it was time someone taught him a lesson.

Time that Bayne taught it.

Spoiling for a fight, Bayne tugged at the hang of his black sack coat, settled his black Stetson atop his thick dark hair, hitched at his black leather gunbelt and then stepped out of his shadowed corner, gently massaging the butts of his Colts with his calloused palms.

He crossed the cave slowly, steadily, not once taking his eyes from the other man. As he walked, his solid-silver spurs jingled distinctively, setting up a weird, discordant tinkle that echoed around the cave.

One by one, the deserters, the miners, the whores and abortionists, the cheats, the road-agents and philanderers the colonel had talked about, all looked around, sensing trouble, that Bayne was restless and on the prod.

He didn't stop walking until his shadow fell across Gorski. The Pole, no longer the big, barrel-chested man he'd once been but still of formidable size, looked up at him. He had a bullet-shaped head and a fuzz of close-cut red-fair hair, a brutal face that had been reshaped by more barrack-room brawls than he could remember. His ears were little more than lumps of dead cartilage, the flesh around his piggy green eyes scarred and constantly swollen.

'*Tak?*' he growled. '*Co czy potrzeba?*'

Bayne felt his temper flare hotter still. Even after all these decades, the sonofabitch still wouldn't address him in English!

'You been lookin' at me again, Gorski,' he said. 'Lookin' at me like you got somethin' on your mind. Well, whatever it is, here's your chance to spit it out or swallow it.'

135

'I got nothin' to say to you,' said Gorski, his accent thick, awkward.

Bayne shook his head. 'Know what? Your tongue says one thing, but your eyes say another.'

Gorski scowled. He had a florid face, a broken nose, big, ugly lips. 'You are callin' me a liar?'

Absolute silence ruled the cavern now, until Bayne growled, 'I'm callin' you a damn' liar.'

Gorski brought his enormous right hand up and scratched thoughtfully at his lantern jaw. He'd broken more than one man with those heavy, scarred fists, but that didn't bother Bayne. Gorski couldn't kill him. Gorski could *never* kill him. But there was a rage building inside him and he had to relieve it or go crazy, so it would be good to let him at least try.

As if reading his mind, Gorski suddenly brought one leg out and around, and Bayne knew a fleeting moment of surprise as his legs were swept out from under him. He went sprawling and Gorski scrambled up, growling like a bear.

Bayne rolled, rose to hands and knees

but knew he was too late. Gorski was already towering over him, one hand grabbing him by the collar, the other by the back of his gunbelt.

A second later Gorski rammed him head-first into the side of the stone altar, and Bayne's neck snapped with a sharp crack.

Bayne swore, rolled over, rocked his head from side to side a couple of times until the broken vertebrae and cartilage clicked back into place, then rose to his feet.

Gorski came thundering towards him, only his eyes showing any emotion. Bayne set himself, brought his fists up and when Gorski was close enough let go a roundhouse right that snapped the Pole's head sideways.

Bayne hit him again, this time in the belly, then sent another jab into his face. Blood wormed from Gorski's right nostril and he stepped back. But that was about the extent of it, so Bayne threw another punch and this time Gorski caught his fist in one big palm and started crushing.

The blood-lust rising in them, the

others quickly formed a ragged circle around them, howling their approval.

Above it all Bayne heard his fingers break and clenched his teeth at the pain, but at the same time he wanted to grin as well because the pain reminded him that he wasn't entirely dead yet, that there were still *some* things he could feel, pain — however fleeting — being one of them.

While Gorski concentrated on pulping his hand, Bayne reached for his left-side Colt and drew it in one smooth motion. He shoved the long, octagonal barrel into Gorski's belly, thumbed back the hammer and fired, once, twice, three times, four.

The force of the bullets sent Gorski flying. He crash-landed on his back, bleeding from the gut, but even as Bayne worked his broken fingers and felt them reset almost instantly, so too did Gorski's wounds stop bleeding and begin to heal.

Bayne ran at Gorski, kicked him in the side and then stamped on his ribcage, cracking his sternum. Gorski roared, grabbed his foot by toe and ankle and snapped it. Again they fell apart; again each man healed within seconds.

Bayne leathered his left-side Colt, drew the right and put a bullet through Gorski's forehead. Gorski's head jerked back, he swayed and then charged forward again and the pair collided, the Pole's weight shoving Bayne hard against the back wall.

Bayne brought his Colt up, intending to put a bullet through Gorski's lower jaw, but Gorski butted him in the face, smearing him with the blood that was still oozing from the wound in his forehead, a wound that was already closing, mending . . .

Bayne almost blacked out but not quite. While he was still disorientated, Gorski grabbed him in a bear-hug, yanked him off his feet, squeezed hard, hard, harder . . .

Bayne's face screwed up as one after another his ribs began to splinter. He tried to break Gorski's hold but couldn't and fired his right-side Colt into the Pole's left foot instead. Blood spurted from Gorski's boot, but still he kept squeezing . . .

Crack . . . crack . . . crack . . .

It didn't matter that these two couldn't hurt each other permanently, that whatever damage one inflicted upon the other would heal within the single blink of a dead red eye; the pain at that moment was almost unbearable.

Bayne's face twisted up even more, his teeth clamped so hard he thought they, too, might splinter. Sweat popped on his forehead, ran down his pitted cheeks.

'Enough!' he screamed at last.

Caught up in the moment, consumed by the need to kill something that was more or less unkillable, Gorski kept squeezing, and Bayne's ribs kept splintering, the ragged ends grating together . . .

'*Enough!*'

The word echoed around the cavern, and this time the watchers fell quiet, sensing with no small satisfaction that if anyone had been taught a lesson, it had been Bayne.

Gorski sensed it too, and finally stopped squeezing. He looked into Bayne's twisted face and then grunted as if at a job well done. He released Bayne and Bayne collapsed at his feet, hugging himself and drawing down great draughts of musty air.

'You don' fight no more, *tak?*' said Gorski, panting.

Bayne didn't look up. He just kept huddled down at Gorski's feet. Finally, he managed: 'No more fight.'

'*Dobrze*,' growled Gorski. He turned away, intending to rejoin the card game.

Big mistake.

The minute his back was turned, Bayne tore his left spur free, and being careful to hold it by its leather strap, came surging back up. Someone — it was that damn' tinhorn, Dolan — yelled a warning: one of the womenfolk screamed.

But before Gorski could react, Bayne leapt onto his broad back, grabbed him around the throat with his right hand and yanked the Pole's big head up. In the same moment he ripped the spur across Gorski's exposed throat, carving a deep, ragged gash.

As soon as the deed was done, Bayne leapt backwards, leaving Gorski to roar and claw at the cut. He blundered around, his roar turning to a weird, bubbling croak as blood filled his throat and then poured down over his fatigue blouse in a crimson cascade.

He then collapsed on his face. And a second after that he vanished in a violent, short-lived burst of white-hot flame.

When the flame folded back in on itself and disappeared, Gorski was gone.

One of the women, a hag who'd once made a good living out of aborting unwanted babies with a mixture of Penny-royal, slippery elm and black cohosh, cried, 'You bastard! You killed him!'

Bayne straightened up, still breathing hard. The fight had invigorated him. For the first time in too long he felt as close to alive as it was possible for a dead man to get.

He faced his accusers and said gloatingly, 'Never occurred to me that my spurs were made of silver.'

'You gutless liar!' said Dolan, stepping forward. 'I remember Charlie Steelgood forging those spurs for you back in '82, out of the hundred silver dollars you gave him!'

Bayne showed him a cold, crooked grin. 'So I forgot.'

'The hell you did!'

Angered not so much by Gorski's death as by Bayne's breaking of a rule that bound them all together, the other vampires began to close their circle around him.

'Killer!' yelled the old abortionist.

The cry immediately was taken up by the others.

'Killer! Killer! Killer!'

Bayne snarled at them, realising at last that there might be consequences to his action that he'd failed to foresee. He backed up, quickly slipped his right spur free, again being careful to hold it by the leather strap, and then brandished it, ready to slash at anyone who came within range.

'Come on, then,' he mocked them. 'Come an' get a taste of eternity!'

He lunged forward and they fell back from him, terrified of the silver spurs and what they could do to vampire flesh. He threw his head back and laughed, enjoying his power, their fear.

But when he looked at them again . . .

A chill washed through him.

They were no longer looking at him, at the spurs.

They were looking at something behind him.

He spun around, saw the colonel framed in the tunnel entrance, saw the fury in the colonel's blue, bead-like eyes and opened his mouth to speak —

Too late.

Max seemed hardly to move. Only the sudden, sharp crack of the snake whip gave any indication that he'd used the weapon at all.

That — and the pain.

It seared through Bayne's shins and calves. He screamed and collapsed, writhing, the spurs falling from his hands as he clutched himself in agony.

The whip had sliced through both legs, cutting his feet off just above the ankles.

Quincy Dolan looked down at him. A cold, deadly smile grazed his lips. 'I always said you needed cutting down to size, Bayne.'

Max coiled the whip slowly, came

forward into the cave with his usual precise footsteps. He looked down at the nearest of Bayne's severed feet, still encased in its boot, and then kicked it toward the sobbing man.

'Try not to put them on backwards,' he said contemptuously. Turning to the others, he added: 'All right! Bayne broke one of our rules and has been punished for it! The rest of you, calm down. We got a full night ahead of us — even you, Bayne. So rest, and rest well, for tonight . . . '

His eyes sparkled in anticipation.

'Tonight,' he cried, 'we feed!'

8

Ed was making his way back to the hotel when he heard the cough and sputter of a poorly-tuned car engine behind him. Turning, he spotted a beat-up, junk-filled VW van bunny-hopping into town. It was covered in gaudy astrological signs that clashed so badly with each other that it made him wince just to look at it.

At the last moment he deliberately crossed the street in front of the van, forcing the driver to slam on his brakes. The man behind the wheel gave him an angry honk and yelled, '*Schmegeggie!*' Without turning, Ed flipped him the finger and walked on, a faint smile showing.

Still annoyed, the VW driver gunned his engine for effect. The engine made an unsavoury grinding sound and backfired, and then once again the van jolted into motion. Ed watched it continue along Main, then make a right onto Fifth.

★   ★   ★

Sam Cocheta entered the Blue Corral Bar about ten minutes later and made straight for the bar. The early evening crowd had yet to appear and the bar was quiet but for a couple of men playing shuffleboard and an undersized hippie-type who was sitting a few stools up, sketching in a notebook. Unless he was very much mistaken, this would be the owner of the garish VW parked outside.

The bartender was leaned against the bar, watching a baseball game on the TV fixed to the back wall. Addressing him, Sam said, 'How's my credit?'

The bartender didn't bother to take his eyes off the screen. 'Used up,' he said.

Expecting as much, Sam allowed himself a philosophical shrug and was about to turn away when the hippie glanced up and said: 'Put it on my tab.'

The bartender shrugged, broke open a bottle of Old Crustacean and set it on the bar. Sam picked it up, turned to his benefactor and toasted him.

'My people have a saying,' he said. 'A

generous man is never without friends.'

'My people have a saying, too. A fool and his money are soon parted.'

'I am Sam Cocheta.'

'You can call me Three-D.'

Three-D was a short, slightly-built fifty year-old: too old, really, for the organic cotton, clay-dyed *Peace* t-shirt, baggy striped cotton pants and stonewashed hemp sneakers he favoured. He had a thin, pleasant face and clear olive skin, a shaggy goatee beard, fuzzy sideburns that extended to his jaw-line and mild brown eyes behind repaired and slightly crooked Aviator sunglasses. His black hair was pulled back in a long pony-tail: atop his head he wore a striped hemp hat with a tightly rolled brim and a stash pocket in which he carried a cell phone.

'A strange name,' Sam said quietly. 'For a strange man, perhaps?'

Three-D smiled briefly. 'Perhaps.'

But as far as Sam was concerned, there was no *perhaps* about it. Behind his glasses, the man's eyes held an alertness and sobriety that was completely at odds with the carefree hippie lifestyle he appeared to follow. He was clearly educated; highly so, Sam suspected; and again this seemed to sit awkwardly with the cluttered Technicolor wreck he drove.

Before he could speculate further, the door opened and they both turned. Ed spotted Three-D at the bar and was just about to go across to him when he also noticed Sam seated nearby. Hesitating, he fixed Sam with a smile and touched his fingers to the brim of his hat before turning and leaving again.

Sam watched the door curiously for a moment. It was impossible to tell what he was thinking. He then nodded to Three-D and left.

* * *

When the VW coughed and growled away from the Blue Corral Bar half an hour later, no one noticed the rattlesnake curled around the rear bumper.

Three-D drove directly to the Place of White Pebbles. Here he pulled off the road and parked in roughly the same spot Gerry Irwin had parked at earlier.

149

He got out, the chill of approaching night making him shiver, then said: 'All right, you can come out now.'

Ed emerged from the back of the van, where he'd hidden among the clutter to avoid being seen by anyone in town.

'Good to see you again, Three-D.' The two old friends shook hands. 'I've got a bad feeling about this one.'

'You and me both.'

'Oh?'

Three-D's full name was David Daniel Da Costa III. He came from a wealthy Jewish family based in Coral Springs, Florida. He had a Ph.D. in Astronomy and Physics, a Ph.D. in Planet and Space Sciences, he'd held high-security clearances at Lockheed, Boeing and Grumman and had even once taught middle-school science.

But, Ed reflected, it had been Three-D's keen interest in the esoteric, plus his exceptional understanding of celestial navigation, astrometry, theoretical astronomy, cosmology, dark matter and the formation and development of the universe that had brought him to the attention of the Seekers, who had eventually recruited him.

All of which meant that when Three-D said he had a bad feeling about something, a wise man took notice.

'Come and take a look at this,' he said. Together they picked a path between the rocks until they reached the spot at which the band had created their pictographs earlier. Still undiscovered, the rattlesnake slowly uncurled from the rear bumper and slithered after them.

It was now full dark, and the white pebbles glowed with a curious phosphorescence. Ed and Three-D traced the outlines of two crescent moons, the sun and finally the four-pointed star.

'Any idea what this is?' Ed asked.

'I'm not sure — yet,' said Three-D. 'But I've seen these symbols somewhere before. I just can't remember where.'

'Maybe some satanic cult?'

'No. Devil-worshippers use the Mark of the Beast, a hexagram — and that has six points. Native Americans, on the other hand . . . they often use four-pointed stars.'

'For . . . ?'

'Well, to the Hopis it represented the

planet Venus, which meant it was time to begin their annual migration. I've seen it on shields and petroglyphs at Willow Springs here in Arizona and at San Cristobal, New Mexico.'

'So this was made by the Hopis?'

'I doubt it. No Hopis around here. But it could signify the time for someone else to migrate.'

'Like who?'

'How the hell should I know? I just happened to run across this place by accident on my way into town.'

'So make a guess.'

Three-D stroked his shaggy goatee as he mulled over his thoughts. He was a short, spry bundle of energy and ideas: Ed often claimed that the Seekers hadn't so much enlisted him as found him in a box marked *G. I. Joe Super Scientist*.

'Moon worshippers?' he said finally.

Ed gave him a withering glance. '*Moon* worshippers? Jeez, Three-D, you've forgotten more than I'll ever know, but the best you can come up with is *Moon* worshippers?'

Three-D muttered a from-the-heart,

'*Shak li ba-tachat!* You asked me to make a guess and I did.'

Hidden among the rocks, Sam Cocheta straightened up off the ground. Focusing his attention on Three-D, he made a series of swift, arcane gestures with his liver-spotted hands.

Simultaneously, Three-D was hit by a new idea. He began to study the tips of the crescent moon a little closer.

Ed stiffened. 'You got something?'

'It's just a hunch,' muttered Three-D. 'But this star *could* represent another planet.'

'Go on.'

'Well, we know the moon is round, that it has no light of its own and merely reflects sunlight. The crescent moon depends upon the angular separation of the moon from the sun as seen from earth — '

'Whoa, whoa, whoa! Back up and talk English, please.'

Three-D sighed. 'I guess this is what I get for hanging out with a *goy* who walks on his knuckles.' Scratching one pebble against another, he added: 'Put simply — what if this *isn't* a representation of our moon? What if it's a moon in another galaxy that really *is* crescent-shaped?'

'Another galaxy? You're talking *Star Trek, chaver.*'

'Have it your way,' Three-D said. 'And it's because I'm your friend that I feel obliged to tell you your pronounciation's terrible. You have to say it like there's an itch at the back of your throat. *Chaver.*'

'*Chaver.*'

'Better.' Three-D tossed one of the pebbles at Ed. 'Tell me why this pebble glows in the dark.'

'Fluorescent paint?'

'That's what I'd have said. But paint comes off when you scratch it hard enough.'

'Hmmm. What does all this have to do with Dead End, anyway?'

'Maybe something, maybe nothing. I really don't know. Like I say, I just happened across it and it struck me as being . . . curious.' He saw Ed glance at his watch and said testily, 'Am I keeping you up?'

'Can the sarcasm, pal. It's just that I've got someplace to be at eight o'clock.'

'Don't tell me — a date?'

'Kind of.'

'*Oy*, you've only been in town twenty-four hours.'

'So I'm a fast worker.'

'Fast? Compared to me you're super-sonic.' He looked once more at the pictographs, saying, 'Well, let's not keep the lady waiting.'

They drove back to town in thoughtful silence, each trying unsuccessfully to piece things together so that they made some kind of sense. Just outside town, Three-D finally brought his disreputable van to a halt and Ed climbed out.

'Sure you won't stay at the hotel?'

'Thanks,' Three-D said. 'But I've got everything I need right here, and the longer people don't know we're in this together, the better chance we have of finding out what's behind this vampire business.'

Ed nodded and said goodnight. But just before the van pulled away again, the rattlesnake slid down off the rear bumper and slithered across to a nearby patch of rocks.

Moments later Sam Cocheta slowly straightened back into human form and stretched to ease his cramped muscles. As he watched Ed walking into town, he took off his Stetson and carefully replaced the snakeskin hatband, which until that moment had been wound around his right wrist. That done, he put the hat back on and strode purposefully into the night.

He was some Indian.

★ ★ ★

Hal Blaylock had never seen the Clubhouse quite so full. The place was packed with townsfolk, most of them dancing energetically to the music of the *Platinum Dead*.

'This is the best turnout we've ever had,' he said, raising his voice to be heard above the sounds of soft rock, laughter and idle chatter. 'I can't thank you enough, Max, for getting those boys to play for us.'

Max shrugged modestly. 'Glad I could do something to make the folks around here happy.'

More than two hundred people had turned up for the dance. Observing the proceedings from one end of the bar, at which patrons could buy non-alcoholic punch or soda, Blaylock was sure it must be some kind of record. And as he looked around the Clubhouse, he felt a justifiable swell of pride.

Although they'd only had a limited budget to work with, his staff had done the community proud. The walls had been covered with silver slash curtains, which shimmered gently beneath the soft mood lighting. A revolving glitter ball cast roving diamonds of white light across the couples smooching on the oak parquet floor. And from the stage at the back of the hall, the *Platinum Dead* were making full use of the Clubhouse's excellent sound facilities in order to entertain the crowd.

Max was pleased with the turnout, too, but for different reasons. His people had been getting increasingly restless. Perhaps the events of tonight would help to settle them down.

He watched Quincy Dolan cross the room. The cadaverous gambler stood a full head taller than most of the people there, which made him hard to miss. His attention, Max saw, was focused on a fair-haired girl standing on the fringes of the dance floor, nursing a glass of cherry Kool-Aid. He thought a moment, then remembered her name: Cathy Maynard.

Dolan passed through the dancers as if they weren't there. When he was near enough, he doffed his hat and said, 'Miss Maynard?'

'Mr Dolan! I didn't expect you to be here tonight.'

'Didn't expect to be here myself, ma'am. I'm not much of a dancer. But it was the hope of finding you here that finally persuaded me to show up.'

She laughed. 'Now, that's a crock if ever I heard one.'

'I call it as I see it, ma'am. And please, call me Quincy.'

She hesitated, then said impulsively, 'Shall we dance, then . . . Quincy?'

'I'd be honoured.'

Fiona stood at the back of the hall, dividing her attention between the performers on stage and the door. Her patience was eventually rewarded when the door swung open and Ed hurried in.

'Where have you been?' she asked as he joined her. 'I tried to reach you at the hotel but Dad said you hadn't come back yet.'

'Sorry, I got hung up. Would you like to dance?'

'I told you I'd save the first one for you.'

'Then let's get to it.'

As they took to the floor, Jake caught Fiona's eye and shook his head in a mixture of disappointment and disapproval. As they danced past, he aimed his guitar at Ed and let go three loud chords, *blang, blang, blang*.

Ed chuckled. 'Lucky that's not a machine gun or I'd be dead by now.'

'Oh, he's harmless enough,' Fiona said. 'In fact, if a girl could dig through all that ego, she'd probably find a pretty nice guy lurking underneath.'

'Are you thinking of digging?'

'I don't have a big enough shovel.'

It was the answer he'd been hoping to hear and he felt relieved. 'How were your patients?'

She looked at him blankly for a moment. 'Excuse me?'

'Your house-calls?'

'Oh. Fine. I'm sorry you didn't get to meet them. Then you'd understand why I love taking care of them.'

'Some other time, maybe.'

Dolan and Cathy Maynard swept past. Ed caught sight of Dolan's distinctive wraparound sunglasses and said, 'What's their story, anyway?'

'The Settlers?' At his nod, she said: 'They showed up out of nowhere about a year ago and leased the mine from the town. Of course, everyone thought they were odd, but no-one would ever tell them that to their faces: it's their money that keeps the town in business.'

'So you try to keep 'em sweet.'

'Absolutely. Dad even arranged these bi-monthly dances after they first moved into the area. He said it was a good way to break down barriers.'

Ed glanced around. 'Looks like he was right.'

Someone tapped him on the shoulder. Turning, he found himself eye-to-eye with

Jake Simms. Pointedly ignoring him, Jake smiled at Fiona, said, 'You owe me a dance, babe.'

Ed's expression tightened and he was just about to tell Jake to get lost when Fiona said, 'And I always pay my debts.'

Before Ed could do or say anything, she and Jake danced away.

'Aren't you afraid the band might hit a sour note without their 'star' up there to guide them?' she said as they danced.

Jake grinned. He moved well and, when he chose to show it, had an irresistible charm that won over most women. 'Not if I don't stay away too long.'

Fiona rolled her eyes. 'I really feel for you, Jake. It must be tough, being so shy.'

'Hey, hot chick like you, in this dump, last thing you need is shy.'

As if to prove his point, he drew her even closer to him.

'Take it easy,' she said. 'I'm partial to breathing.'

His grin widened. 'Aren't we all?'

★ ★ ★

Just beyond the town limits, a faint, grinding rumble began to roll in off the desert. Slowly, steadily it built in volume. Finally a set of headlights showed through the darkness, followed by another, and another, then several more.

A silver Chevy Tahoe appeared beneath the sodium lights strung along Main, followed by a second. In their wake came two Mack trucks hauling flatbed or step-deck trailers, the trailers carrying — among other things — tarpaulin-covered Caterpillar excavators and dozers.

Two Kenworth 8×4 dump trucks came next, then three silver panel vans, two silver cargo vans and lastly, a silver Van Hool motor-coach.

The leading vehicles turned right off Main and headed directly for the Sunrise Motel. The rest followed suit. Soon the weed-choked parking lot was full.

When it came to a halt, some twenty men and women climbed out of the motor-coach. Unsupervised, they immediately went to work, inspecting the equipment contained in the cargo vans, making sure it had withstood the journey and that everything was present and correct. Several of them wore the white coats of lab technicians.

The two SUVs disgorged a curious variety of people. Some appeared to be businessmen in sharp, expensive suits. Others wore police uniforms. Two were junior officers in the US Army.

Standing outside the dismal front office, Pete Johnson and Roy Drake exchanged grins.

CATLIN CONSTRUCTION had just come to town.

★ ★ ★

Jake felt someone tap him on the shoulder. He stopped dancing, as did Fiona, turned and saw Ed standing behind him.

'Time's up, pal.'

Jake recognised the challenge and was about to rise to it when Fiona gave his arm a distracting squeeze. When he looked at her, she said, 'I think I just heard that sour note.'

He grinned, thanked her for the dance

then shouldered past Ed on his way back to the stage.

As Ed took Fiona in his arms, he said, 'Did I come back too soon?'

'Jake? He helped me get my car started this morning. But . . . '

'What?'

'He *is* cute.'

'Well, that certainly sets my mind at rest.'

He had the feeling he was being watched. When he glanced around, he saw Max watching him intently from the bar. 'You know, I don't think your dad likes me much.'

'That's curiosity, not dislike,' she said. 'He's wondering what it is about you that made me change my mind.'

'About what?'

'I don't usually come to these dances, Ed. And when I do I tend to keep strictly to myself.'

'I'd be flattered — if I hadn't already seen the local competition.'

As the night wore on, Fiona grew more comfortable in his company. She became more affectionate too, and was nibbling gently at his earlobe when she confessed, 'I think I've finally figured you out.'

'Oh? Tell me, so we'll both know.'

'You're a wolf in sheep's clothing.'

His eyes narrowed and for a moment his mood sobered. 'A wolf, huh?'

'Uh-huh.'

'You're kidding, right? You don't really think I'm dangerous?'

'I do.'

'Why?'

'You've got this mysterious edge . . . It's not a bad thing. In fact, I realise now that it's what attracted me to you in the first place, but — '

'You talk too much,' he said, and was about silence her with a kiss when the room was plunged into darkness.

Simultaneously, the band's instruments fell silent. Dancers stopped dancing and began asking each other what had happened.

Jake and the rest of the band already knew.

Fiona glanced across Ed's shoulder. Even though the room was in near-total darkness, she was able to see her father as clearly as if it had been filled with daylight. He beckoned to her.

'I'll meet you at the exit,' she told Ed. Before he could object, she was gone.

She weaved between couples until she reached Max's side. He leaned close and whispered something to her. She shook her head and began to object, but one glance from him silenced her. Head bowed, she submissively walked away. He watched her go with a troubled scowl.

As the stewards started switching on flashlights, Hal Blaylock got up on the stage and appealed for order. 'Sorry, folks,' he said. 'Guess we forgot to pay our electric bill.'

Everyone laughed.

'Seriously, though,' he continued, 'there seems to have been a power failure.'

'Can you fix it?' asked someone in the crowd.

'Not tonight. But we'll make it up to you next time we have a dance. Free dinner for all?'

The audience roared their approval and then reluctantly began to make their way toward the now torch-lit exit.

Blaylock turned to Jake and the others and offered his hand. 'Sorry about the blackout, boys. But again, thanks for coming. If there's ever anything I can do for you — '

'There is,' said Jake. 'We'd like to rent the high school gym for about a week. Some music execs are coming to hear our new songs and we need a place to practice. Can you swing that?'

'Sure. Least I can do. I'll run it by the council, but with the kids on vacation I don't see any problem. Come by my office tomorrow and we'll work out the details.'

★ ★ ★

Fiona was waiting for Ed when he came outside. Around them, townsfolk and Settlers both were taking their leave, many in pairs and holding hands. Ed noticed the gambler and the fair-haired girl among them. In fact, now that he thought about it, he realised that a lot of the Settlers seemed to have hooked up with townspeople tonight.

167

They were about to get into Fiona's SUV when Jake saw them from across the street, where he'd been asked to sign autographs for a small group of local girls. Seeing her with Ed, he said incredulously: 'You're taking *him* over me?'

Fiona laughed. 'You were never in the running, 'babe.''

Jake mimed being stabbed in the heart and staggered a couple of paces. Fiona threw him a wave, then climbed into the SUV and drove them away.

After a minute or so Ed said, 'This isn't the way to the hotel.'

'No,' she agreed. 'But it *is* the way to my place.'

*   *   *

Jake went back to signing autographs. He'd always loved an audience and now took great delight in trading banter with his adoring public.

He'd just finished signing his name with a particular flourish when he felt something — some*one* — soft and warm push against his right arm.

He turned and saw a good-looking girl in her mid-twenties smiling up at him. She had blue eyes and an inviting smile, and a single white streak running back from her left temple to vanish into her otherwise blonde hair. She looked vaguely familiar and so did her red and black satin dress. For a moment he couldn't figure out why. Then it hit him: she was the crazy wild chick in Ed's hotel room — the one who had leaped out the window and landed on her feet in the street below. The challenge of taming her appealed to him and he turned on his charm.

'Hey, gorgeous.'

'Hey,' said Wanda.

'You want my autograph?'

She shook her head and mouthed: '*I want you.*'

His raised one eyebrow. 'Is that a fact?' he said, grinning smugly. 'I *think* that could be arranged.'

★ ★ ★

It was a little after midnight when the tour bus pulled up in front of the hotel. The door shushed open and Kyle, Brad and Beau climbed out and made straight for the lobby.

There was no sign of Jake.

Gerry Irwin squeezed out from behind the wheel and looked back along the darkened bus. Jake had fetched along a passenger, a blonde girl he'd taken straight into his own personal sleeping area. It was easy to imagine what was happening in there now.

Gerry shook his head, suddenly depressed and in need of a drink he knew he dare not have. Nothing had changed over the years. He'd started out on this life because he'd thought it might help him meet girls. And here he was, almost twenty years on, still trying to meet them.

For a moment he debated whether or not to knock and tell Jake that they'd arrived, but he doubted that he'd appreciate the interruption. Instead he climbed down off the bus and closed the door behind him. Let them have their fun. He should be glad that *someone*, at least, was getting a little.

Wanda kept Jake so fully occupied that he wasn't even aware that the bus had slowed to a halt. The minute he'd closed the sliding door behind them she'd pushed him down onto the narrow bed and draped herself on top of him, kissing, nibbling, stroking, squeezing — the whole nine yards. My God, it was like she couldn't get enough of him.

He'd been just as bad. He'd torn the straps of her sexy red satin dress down off her creamy shoulders, flipped the full skirt up in order to feel her legs and butt, then closed his fingers around her thong and dragged it down to her ankles.

Now Wanda broke away from him, but only so that she could straddle him more comfortably. He went willingly, muttering his approval, and when she started grinding herself against him he threw his head back, just as she'd been hoping he would, and revealed the long, slender column of his neck and the veins that throbbed and pulsed there.

In the darkness Wanda's eyes began to glow red.

'Oh baby,' breathed Jake. 'Come on, baby, don't keep me waiting . . . '

Her lips peeled back and she thought, *I won't. I won't keep you waiting any longer than I have to.*

In the next moment she struck.

She buried her mouth into his throat and bit him, hard. Beneath her Jake stiffened and groaned.

Blood spurted from the bite into her face.

Orange blood.

Orange?

She recoiled, staggered to her feet and spat off to one side, her eyes going wide.

Poison!

She stumbled away from him, confused and scared, and tore the sliding door open. She lurched outside, already choking and clawing at her throat. She felt as if she were on fire. Everything was tingling, she was feeling hot, then cold, then hot again.

Finally she reached the exit door. Pushing it open she started down the steps, almost falling in her hurry to escape.

Somehow maintaining her balance, she staggered on, wheezing now, and wandered off into the night.

★ ★ ★

In the bus Jake lay on his bed exactly where she'd left him, his throat a mess, his black eyes staring sightlessly toward the ceiling.

But then a very curious thing happened.

The wound at his throat began to move somehow, the ragged edges oozing slowly together until they were finally sealed. There came a soft bubbling hiss as the flesh knitted back together, leaving no scar. Immediately, Jake's sightless eyes cleared and he sat up and blinked.

He remembered what Brad had said about Wanda the previous night and grinned.

Man, that is one tough chick.

9

Parked out in the desert, Three-D had set up his NexStar 8 telescope beside the van and was gazing thoughtfully at the stars.

He had no idea that he was being watched from the surrounding shadows by the very same rattlesnake that had accompanied him to the Place of White Pebbles.

After a while he straightened up to ease the aches in his back. He reached into the van for a Bud, took a swig and sighed. He was mildly frustrated. To call this business a conundrum was putting it mildly, he decided. Usually his trained analytical mind had little problem in figuring out the facts of a matter, regardless of how obscure or arcane those facts might be. But this time . . .

Well, much as he hated to admit it, he was fresh out of ideas.

Until, that was, the rattler suddenly fixed him with an intense, unblinking stare.

For an infinitesimal moment Three-D seemed to freeze as a new idea suggested itself to him. He thought about it for a moment more, then quickly settled himself in the VW's passenger seat and typed something into his laptop.

Light from the screen threw the shadows of his nose and brows back up across his face as he scrolled down, absorbing the data through questing eyes.

The screen was filled with diagrams and data relating to stars, planets and solar systems. He hit a few more keys and a few seconds later the screen filled with images of the ancient Anasazi cliff dwellings in Canyon de Chelly, a national monument a little over a hundred miles to the northeast.

Several of the rock drawings scattered throughout the region depicted two crescent moons, one upside down with a sun below it, the other with a star juxtaposed similarly to the layout they'd seen earlier at the Place of White Pebbles.

Yes! he thought. *That's where I saw it!*

He grabbed his cell phone, punched in a number.

There was no reply.

Come on, Ed, pick it up . . . la' azazel itcha!

But Ed didn't.

The rattler slithered off into the night.

★   ★   ★

All through town the vampires fed.

In her ten year-old Hyundai Accent, Cathy Maynard and Quincy Dolan enjoyed a passionate embrace until at length Dolan drew back from her and looked her directly in the eyes.

His grew red.

Hers quickly glazed over.

While she was in this hypnotic state, he bent his face to her throat and fed, being careful to take just enough blood to satisfy his appetites and no more.

Throughout Dead End it was much the same story. The vampires fed from the humans they had befriended at the dance. Rendered unconscious, the humans offered no resistance. And as with Dolan, each vampire took only enough blood for his or her needs.

The colonel had taught them that these people were a resource, and a precious one at that. And because they need never even guess that their blood had been harvested in such a way, it could and would be harvested again and again at regular bi-monthly intervals.

★   ★   ★

The phone in Ed's jacket pocket buzzed a few times more, then fell silent. The jacket itself lay where it had been discarded on Fiona's living room floor. His hat lay nearby, too.

Fiona lived in a modest, ranch-style house a few miles outside town. He'd had just enough time to notice its long, low profile, the fact that it was L-shaped, with adobe walls and rustic white porch posts, and then the electricity that had been sparking between them all evening suddenly went into overload.

Now they were in the bedroom, sprawled across the bed and kissing passionately, and Ed was so caught up in the moment that he had no clear memory of how they'd gotten there from the car.

Fiona grabbed him by the hair and pushed his head sideways so that she could cover his exposed neck with an urgent flurry of steamy kisses. The heat of his blood and the closeness of his jugular were almost impossible to resist. She closed her lids to hide eyes that had turned red and as she continued to nuzzle him and listen to the soft moans he made in return, she opened her mouth, felt her fangs begin to lengthen and knew that, at last, this was the moment.

But still she hesitated.

Could she do it?

Could she?

Did she even *want* to do it to this of all men?

What are you waiting for? her father's voice asked inside her head. *Bite him!*

She was tempted. Oh so sorely tempted.

But . . .

No. No, father, I won't!

Ed, kissing her neck in return, sensed her hesitancy and drew back to look her in the face. He couldn't see much in the darkness, but saw enough to know that she was clearly troubled by something, and close to tears.

'What's wrong?' he asked.

Before she could reply, there came a vague stir of movement from the corner behind her. Ed sat up quickly as Max ghosted out of the darkness, in uniform now and glaring at him through crimson eyes.

'What — ?'

Ed tried to push Fiona aside and get to his feet, but one look from those red eyes paralysed him, and all he could do was watch as Max — a demonic version of the seemingly good-natured Max with whom he was more familiar — came closer.

As if from a great distance he heard Fiona cry, 'Father, no!'

Max fixed her with an equally fierce glower. 'Bring him to the mines!' he ordered.

'No!'

'Do it or I'll destroy you!'

'No!'

He shook his head at her. 'Do you *really* want to end up like your mother?'

he said before he could stop himself.

The room grew very quiet.

'M-My mother?' said Fiona, her voice small now. 'She died of cholera. You said so your — '

He looked away from her, unwilling to meet her gaze. 'That's right,' he murmured.

But the damage had already been done, the seed of doubt sown. Looking up at him she said, 'You lied to me, didn't you? About her?'

He opened his mouth to voice some kind of denial, then saw the futility in it and changed his mind. 'She gave me no choice,' he said. 'She was going to leave me and take you with her. I warned her not to, but she wouldn't listen — '

'So you destroyed her, too?'

He looked at her, said dully, 'I had to.'

Instantly, Fiona sprang up off the mattress and threw herself at him, punching at his chest with her balled fists. 'Liar! Liar! *Liar!*'

Moving with incredible speed, he grabbed and held her wrists, his fury rushing back to the surface. 'I told you, I had no choice! She defied me once too often, her and her cursed human sentimentality!'

He drew himself up, hissed, 'Now do as I say. Bring him to the mines!'

She returned his glare without flinching, tightened her mouth defiantly.

'*Do it!*' he screamed. This time she actually cringed, and with good reason. For as he lost his temper completely, everything animalistic about him suddenly reappeared; his alabaster skin stretched back across his skull, his brow and cheekbones thrust forward, his eyes sank deeper into his head, there to glow like burning rubies, and his fangs . . .

They seemed to lengthen still more, and to Ed they looked as if they'd been fashioned from silver.

Cowed now, Fiona nodded and turned to Ed, picking him up as if he were weightless. Ed felt his stomach clench tight. Too late he was finally starting to make sense of this business — and now, he realised, there wasn't a damn' thing he could do about it.

*   *   *

Out at the Place of White Pebbles, Sam Cocheta sat cross-legged in the centre of the four-pointed star. Naked to the waist, he used an old Apache hunting knife to cut several long gashes in his chest. Only the smallest flexing of the muscles around his mouth and eyes hinted at the pain they caused.

That done, he set the knife aside, dipped the tips of his fingers into the cuts and then smeared the blood across his lined face. Finally he rose to his feet, took up a small elk-hide drum upon which had been painted what looked like a four-bladed airplane propeller. In fact it was a depiction of the four winds, which in turn symbolised the winds of change.

He began to dance around the outline of the star, flicking blood onto the white pebbles as he went.

*   *   *

'You're sure he never returned from the dance?'

182

The duty clerk at the Vickers House felt himself wilting before the urgency of Three-D's gaze, and nodded. 'Absolutely, sir.'

To his immense relief Three-D finally turned away, deep in thought. His VW has squealed to a halt out front barely half a minute earlier, and mere seconds later the little ball of energy had burst into the lobby, his presence surprisingly large and almost overwhelming.

At last Three-D turned back to the clerk and said: 'All right. 'When he does, have him call me.'

'Yes, sir.'

'And tell him it's urgent!'

★　★　★

The vampires started returning to the mine a little before sunrise. They came in twos and threes, blood staining their lips and teeth. But there was nothing predatory about them now. If anything they appeared quiet, exhausted, satisfied.

They entered the mine and made their way along the dark, maze-like tunnels, past the discarded bones of the cholera victims, disturbing rats from the piles as they went. When they reached the cavern, they found Max and Fiona already waiting for them — and a brown-haired man in jeans and a creased white shirt stretched out on the altar.

Immediately the vampires' interest sharpened, even that of Bayne, who had fallen into a moody silence after being punished by the colonel. Who was this new victim and why had the colonel elected to bring him here?

Sensing their curiosity, Max ran his eyes over them and urged them to gather around.

Watching them, Ed felt as if he were trapped in a nightmare. Suddenly he was surrounded by pale, blood-smudged faces. Here he recognised Charlie Steelgood, there the tall, cadaverous gambler he'd seen earlier. And there, his expression especially cold, the black-clad man with the horseshoe moustache and silver spurs.

Damn! Try as he might, there was nothing he could do to escape either their scrutiny or their clutches. Although feeling was returning slowly, he was still to all intents and purposes paralysed.

'I want you to see this,' Max said at last. His harsh, cold voice bounced off the rough walls. 'I want you to see how the blood of my blood deals with the humans when there is no need to spare them.'

A murmur of appreciation rustled through the gathering. Anticipation began to shine in their red eyes.

'Fiona?'

Her voice was tiny. 'Yes, father.'

Max smiled. 'He's yours.'

She looked from his face to Ed's. She looked scared and close to tears, the victim of some terrible inner struggle that could only have one outcome: the *wrong* one. She knew she dare not disobey her father now, not before the others. If she did, he would throw her to them to do with as they would, if only to show them the terrible penalty for disobedience.

She drew closer. The crowd parted to let her approach the altar. She came around to the far side, looking down at Ed and trying to ignore her human side, the side that wanted to cry and rebel against this horror.

She closed her eyes. Her eyelids fluttered as the skin slowly began to glow red. When she opened them again Ed was shocked to see that they were a burning scarlet. She reached down, tore his shirt open, and a low, anticipatory sigh went through her audience. She opened her mouth impossibly wide, and was just about to bring her head down upon his throat when —

'P-please . . . h-help me . . . '

As one, the gathered vampires heeled toward the cavern entrance, through which Wanda had just stumbled.

His anger rising again, Max demanded, 'What is it? What's the matter?'

Before she could reply, Wanda's eyes suddenly rolled up into her head and she collapsed.

Swaying with relief at the temporary reprieve, Fiona stepped back and hurried across to the fallen girl. She knelt and cradled Wanda's head in her lap, leaning close so that she could hear what the girl was trying to say.

Wanda's voice gurgled briefly and then

a tremor passed through her. Abruptly she stiffened and fell still. Frowning, Fiona carefully set her head down, then stood up and looked at her father.

'She bit one of the band-members,' she said, clearly puzzled. 'Jake. But she says his blood wasn't . . . '

'Well?' Max urged when she fell quiet.

'She says it wasn't *human.*'

Ethan Bayne looked from daughter to father. 'What the hell does that mean, not human?' he growled.

'She said it was orange, that it tasted *bitter.*'

Without warning, Wanda's body suddenly ignited. There was a brief flash of pure white flame which disappeared almost immediately, and when it was gone, so too was Wanda.

Silence filled the cavern, until Ed, regaining some of his faculties at last, croaked, 'Looks like you've got a . . . problem, Max.'

Max wheeled around. Ed had propped himself on his elbows and now tried his best to meet the other man's powerful red stare.

'What do *you* know about this?' Max hissed.

In truth, Ed knew practically nothing. But having regained his senses at last, he realised that escape from this place was impossible — unless he somehow managed to convince Max that he and the rest of these creatures needed him.

Swallowing dryly he said, 'There's some strange markings out in the desert. Maybe they're alien.'

'What's that to us?'

'Maybe everything — if they're hostile.'

A frown settled across the bony ridge of Max's brow. 'Why should that trouble us? The humans are our enemies. It's you who seek to destroy us. Why should we care what aliens do to *you?*' He flicked a glance at Charlie Steelgood and barked, 'Chain him!'

Fiona cried, 'No!'

She came at him in a rush, but he backhanded her away and sent her sprawling to the floor.

It was the final straw.

As she pushed back to her feet, Fiona was in full vampire mode, and anything about her that was once even remotely human had been replaced by all that was bestial.

She fixed Max with a hateful vermillion glare and began to advance upon him, and Max said with just a hint of alarm, 'Back off! Don't make me hurt you!'

She shook her head in disgust. 'It's too late for that,' she snarled. 'You've already hurt me more than you know.'

She was a blur as she threw herself at him again, but Max still managed to catch her in mid-air and then fling her away from him. With a scream of rage she flew backwards, the scream ending abruptly when she slammed into the cavern wall and then pitched forward onto the ground.

Determinedly she shoved back to her feet, but Max was already there, standing over her, just waiting to grab her by the shoulders, hoist her off her feet and throw her again, this time at the opposite wall.

Although she landed in a bruised heap long before she could hit it, it was obvious that she was already weakening.

Weakened or not, though, she came back up and hurled herself at him again, bearing her teeth, scratching furiously with her nails, and for a moment she fought with such intensity that she actually drove him back beneath her onslaught.

But Max was only biding his time. Moving so fast that Ed never even saw it, he backhanded his daughter away and she crashed to the floor, rolled, lay on her belly for a moment, trying to get her breath back.

Max intended to give her no such opportunity. Again he moved faster than a human eye could follow, and then, all at once, he was looming above her again. He grabbed her one-handed around the neck, raised her up, up, higher, until she was suspended at arm's-length, her legs kicking, her face screwed tight with the effort it took to still draw breath.

Gradually her struggles grew weaker, even more ineffectual. Max bellowed for her to give up, that she could never win. And then, when she summoned the strength to grab his wrist in her hands and try to make him release his hold,

Max saw that he had no choice but to turn the full intensity of his vampiric glare upon her.

Ed winced, watching as her eyes widened to become twin red pools of pure, undiluted fear. A split second later the light went out of them and she hung loose and unresponsive in her father's grasp.

He felt like weeping when Max tossed her aside.

* * *

To the dismay of her patients, Fiona's receptionist taped a sign to the surgery door early the following morning that said *DR VICKERS WILL NOT BE IN TODAY*.

'I'm sorry, folks,' she said. 'But even doctors get sick sometimes.'

That cut little ice with the pale, haggard-looking patients who packed the waiting room. 'Well, when *will* she be in?' asked one.

'Her father didn't say. He just called and said Fiona wouldn't be here today.'

'But I have to see her,' moaned one of the male patients. 'We *all* do . . . '

'I've got a baby to look after,' said Cathy Maynard. 'But right now I'm so weak I can barely even walk.'

'I'm sorry,' said the receptionist. 'Maybe tomorrow.'

As she turned and hurried back to the relative protection of her counter, the patients traded looks. An elderly woman fanned herself and muttered, 'I've lived here all my life and I've never suffered mosquito bites like these . . . '

The others could only mutter their agreement. They hadn't, either.

★   ★   ★

Work on the demolition of the Sunrise Motel was well underway. Already more than half of the structure had been flattened and the Caterpillars were scooping up the debris and dropping it into the dump trucks for removal.

The site was a hive of activity. Lab technicians were busy checking the banks of equipment they'd set up the previous night, checking cables, noting readings and flipping switches. Although few people would ever know it, it was the vast amount of power needed to work these state-of-the-art computer banks that had caused last night's blackout.

On the far side of the parking lot, Pete Johnson paused for a moment to watch his men checking the equipment in the three panel vans. He clambered up into the back of one to take a look for himself.

The vans were packed with long matt green crates. Taking a screwdriver from his tool belt, he prised up the lid of the nearest box and inspected its contents.

The box contained factory-new ArmaLite AR-15 assault rifles; what the military called the M16.

He checked another box. This one held FGM-148 Javelin 'fire-and-forget' portable anti-tank guided-missile launchers.

A third crate contained M79 40 × 46mm grenade launchers.

Other crates contained ammunition for them all.

He hopped down from the van and smiled. There was enough material here to fight a whole new war, and that was just as well, because a whole new war was coming.

His cell phone buzzed. He checked the caller ID, answered it and listened a moment. When he ended the call he glanced around, spotted Roy Drake and beckoned him over.

'News?' asked Drake.

Johnson nodded. 'Spread the word,' he said softly. 'Tonight at six-thirty. The high school gymnasium.'

10

Deep in the Stygian depths of the mine, time lost all meaning. To Ed, the fight between Max and Fiona seemed as if it had taken place weeks ago and that he'd spent at least twice that long chained by the wrists to a large support beam at the back of the cavern.

He knew that couldn't be so. The almost total darkness and the after-effects of whatever weird, paralysing power Max had zapped him with were playing tricks on his mind. More likely it was just a matter of hours, probably no more than five or six, but it seemed longer because of the awkward, half-crouching position he'd been forced to adopt at the end of the short chain.

The mine was cold and damp, and he was shivering. To take his mind off the discomfort, he tried to put together everything he'd learned so far — which admittedly wasn't much — and make sense of it.

Max was at the centre of Dead End's vampire problem. The Settlers weren't some old-fashioned religious group, as they claimed. They were vampires whose beginnings could be traced all the way back to the days of the Old West; maybe longer.

And Fiona . . .

He let go a hard sigh.

Even though she'd tried to protect him — even to the point of defying her father — Fiona was a vampire, too. And that put them firmly on opposite sides of the fence.

The cloying near-silence was oppressive, especially mixed as it was with the almost impenetrable darkness. He didn't want to lose control of himself, knowing he was finished if he did, but it was hard not to panic. All around the cavern the vampires had found niches in which to sleep through the hours of daylight. He was surrounded by them, by creatures who lived even though they had been dead for at least a hundred and thirty years.

It wasn't the kind of revelation designed to comfort or console.

He was still trying to figure a way out of his predicament when he sensed movement nearby. He caught his breath. A moment later someone snuck up beside him, drawing so close that he could smell the faint traces of her perfume through the gloom and knew that it was Fiona.

He didn't know whether to be glad her father hadn't destroyed her, as he'd feared, or to brace himself for the inevitable, throat-ripping bite he was sure must come.

'If you've come to gloat,' he whispered, 'save your breath.'

Fiona kept her own voice at a similar level. 'You can hate me later. Right now we have to get you out of here.'

He was going to reply with some half-hearted show of bravado but before he could, she took hold of the chain in both her hands and pulled. Slowly the links began to stretch like warm taffy, before finally snapping apart. He looked at her in disbelief. Incredibly, Fiona hadn't even broken a sweat.

He collapsed to the floor, weakly massaging his wrists. When at last he found his voice again, he said: 'I don't know what you're up to, but — '

'You talk too much,' she said, and kissed him.

Only the sound of Ethan Bayne, sleeping lightly in a niche a short distance away, forced her to end their embrace. Taking him by the hand, she helped him to his feet and led him silently across the cavern, picking a slow, painstaking path between all the sleeping bodies.

At length they made it to the mouth of a tunnel in the left-side wall, and Fiona began to move a little faster. Despite the beating she'd taken she seemed tireless, and it was all he could do to keep up with her. She tried to get him to jog, but at first the best his cramped limbs could muster was a painful kind of shuffle.

'Why aren't you asleep like the others?' he asked as he limped along behind her.

When she made no reply, he surprised her by stopping dead in his tracks and yanking her back towards him. 'I'm not moving again until you tell me,' he said.

She looked at him in the darkness, her night vision allowing her to see that he wasn't bluffing. 'Because the daylight has no effect on me,' she said at last.

'Even without those wraparound sun-glasses?'

'No.'

'Why not?'

'I'm three-quarters human. My mother was human, my father's half-human. But his vampire side rules.'

'And yours?'

'I'm helping you escape, aren't I?' She threw a glance back the way they'd come, then said, 'Come on, we've got to hurry.'

'Where are we going?'

'This tunnel leads straight to my house,' she explained. 'It's the way we brought you here last night, but you were out of it at the time.'

'I'm not much better now.'

'You're still alive, aren't you? Look,' she said, 'you can whine all you like later. Right now we have to get out of here! If my father finds us again, I won't be able to stop him from killing you.'

He looked at her for a beat, said quietly, 'Since you put it that way — let's move it.'

★   ★   ★

In Hal Blaylock's office, the Mayor said, 'I haven't seen him, either. The last time I saw Ed he was leaving the dance with Dr Vickers.'

'Where's her office?' demanded Three-D.

'On Main Street. But she's not there today. Do you think it's worth trying her house?'

'Can you give me directions?'

'I'll do better than that. I'll take you there myself. After all, Fiona's the reason I called the Seekers in the first place.'

'Oh?'

'Half the people around here have bite marks on their throat and are staggering around like they need a blood transfusion. Her diagnosis? That we've all been bitten by mosquitoes.'

'Do you have any special reason to doubt her? I mean, she is a doctor.'

Blaylock stood up and loosened his bolo tie so that he could open the neck of his shirt and pull back the collar. 'Do these look like mosquito bites to you?'

Three-D paled visibly. '*Ben zonah!* When did you get those?'

'Last night. And I've felt crappy ever

since.' He snatched up a pair of Bolle sunglasses. 'Had to wear these just to step out in the sun. And when I got back from breakfast, it was all I could do not to find a dark corner someplace and go to sleep.'

Three-D looked him in the eye. 'You know what that could mean? For you and the others? In the long-term?'

'Sure,' said Blaylock, readjusting his tie. 'Why do you think I contacted the Seekers? Dead End's got enough vampires as it is. The last thing we need around here is any more!'

*　*　*

For a long while all they did — all they *could* do — was run, and then, when Fiona sensed that Ed was starting to flag again, slow to a resolute kind of trot until he could catch his second wind. The tunnel was dark, narrow, claustrophobic. The air was cold and very slightly tainted. The harsh saw of Ed's breathing was thrown back at him in loud, panting echoes.

Gradually the tunnel narrowed even more and after about a hundred yards it

201

came to a dead end. Here a rusted metal ladder was bolted to the dark facing wall. Fiona went first, climbing like a cat. She pushed up through some kind of trap door and Ed immediately felt a wash of fresh air that put new life into him. He followed her up through the trap and found himself in her utility room.

'We can't stay here,' Fiona said, more to herself than to him. 'It's the first place my father will look for you.'

'Well, I'm not leaving town, if that's what you're after. I'm not finished here yet.'

He went into the living room and scooped up his jacket, reached into the pocket and took out his cell phone. As he speed-dialled Three-D's number, he went through to the kitchen, opened the fridge door and looked inside. He spotted a can of juice and helped himself.

At last Three-D answered the call. It sounded as if he were in his van and on the move. 'Goddammit, *chaver*, where've you been?' he demanded. 'Are you okay?'

'I'm fine,' Ed said. 'Where are you?'

'With the Mayor. He's driving me out

to Dr Vickers' house — '

'That's where I am right now! With Fiona — '

'Then get out of there fast!' Three-D barked urgently. 'She might be — '

'I know. But don't worry, I'm okay. How about you? Did you find anything?'

Three-D drew a breath. 'Those astro bodies outlined by white pebbles? They're similar to some of the Anasazi pictographs at Canyon de Chelly.'

Ed swallowed the last of the juice. 'So what are you saying? The pebbles were put there by ancient cliff-dwellers?'

'No. They'd have been found long before now, if that were the case. This pebble layout is recent.'

'So who did it? Any idea?'

'I can make a guess, but it means taking another visit to *Star Trek* country.'

'All right, I'm listening.'

'Aliens who migrated here around the time of the Anasazi and are now ready to return to their own planet,' said Three-D.

Ed considered that. 'Suppose you're right. Why here, and why are they leaving now?'

'Beats me. But if you're interested in coincidences, the latest pictures from the Hubbell showed a bunch of new dwarf galaxies beyond Dwingeloo One — '

'What the hell's Dwingeloo One?'

'*Shoteh!* A barred spiral galaxy in the Zone of Avoidance that's obscured by the Milky Way.'

'Aw, get off the fucking podium, Three-D!'

'Bottom line,' said Three-D, 'the aliens' planet is in one of those dwarf galaxies and it's now aligned with earth so that it's possible to travel back there — '

Just then the back door broke open with a splintery crack and Fiona cried out, 'Father!'

Even as Ed turned, Max stormed into the kitchen and fixed him with eyes that rapidly turned from blue to pink to orange to red, and it was all Ed could do to keep standing. The phone dropped from his nerveless hand, hit the kitchen floor with Three-D's tiny, tinny voice saying, 'Ed? *Chaver?* You still there? Answer me!'

Max came deeper into the room. Fiona

quickly stepped in front of Ed and faced her father. Though half-human, he was all-vampire as he continued to pin Ed with his crimson gaze and work his lower jaw from side to side in anticipation of the blood-letting to come.

'Father . . . please, leave him alone.'

Max ignored her.

Ed backed up until his back pressed against the fridge and he realised with a sinking feeling that he couldn't go any farther. Fear tightened his throat so that it was hard to talk. But he knew he had to at least try. Talking was all he had right now: if it came to blows he was finished for sure.

'Before you kill me,' he gasped, 'hear me out. I was right. There *are* aliens here.'

Max continued to advance, his eyes bright with the killing lust.

Desperately Ed made another stab at it. 'You say you're not interested in what they'll do to us, but you should be.'

Max reached him, flashed out one hand, grabbed his shirtfront, lifted and then threw him. Ed hit the wall by the door, slid down in a heap on the living room carpet, shook his head and kept talking, his voice desperate now.

'If they're hostile and plan to wipe us out, or maybe even take us with them when they leave . . . '

Max towered over him, grabbed him by the hair, twisted until Ed's face screwed tight and then lifted him up off his feet.

Fiona screamed, 'Father, please! You've got to listen to him!'

' . . . you'll lose your supply of blood,' Ed managed.

At the word blood, a new emotion entered Max's blazing red eyes. Without warning, he released his grip and Ed fell to his knees. Somehow he found the strength to struggle to his feet and stood swaying before the vampire leader.

'Which means you and the rest of your clan are living on borrowed time,' he finished.

The light in Max's eyes began to fade, revert from red to orange to pink to blue, and the skin across his face seemed to relax, so that the bony ridges grew less pronounced. After a moment he said,

'You're lying! Right now you'd say anything to save yourself.'

'That's true enough. But what if I'm not, Max? Can you afford to take that risk?'

The sound of a car squealing to a halt outside broke the silence. Fiona hurried to the window and looked out. 'It's the Mayor, and someone I've never seen before.'

'That'll be my partner,' said Ed. 'Three-D. He'll verify everything I've said.'

Footsteps clattered up the path, followed a moment later by a furious hammering at the front door. Ed kept his eyes locked on Max's. Over the clamour he said as reasonably as he could, 'All I'm asking for is a temporary truce.'

'If he's right,' added Fiona, 'and you do nothing, you'll be responsible for the death of our entire race!'

'And if I'm wrong,' said Ed, 'you can always kill me later.'

Grudgingly Max allowed his human form to take over completely. 'Let them in,' he said quietly.

★ ★ ★

That, of course, was just the first step. The second was to get everyone to sit down and put all the pieces together. The third was most difficult — to get them all to believe it.

When Ed finished speaking, Hal Blaylock said, '*Aliens?* Are you trying to tell me that everyone around here is being bitten by *aliens?*'

Ed glanced at Max and Fiona before saying: 'No. This has nothing to do with the bites. This is another problem entirely.'

'A *potential* problem,' Three-D reminded him. 'We don't have any proof yet. But it wouldn't hurt to ask around town and find out if anyone's seen anything unusual lately.' He took out the sketch he'd made of the pictographs they'd found out at the Place of White Pebbles. 'How about this? Does it look at all familiar?'

Max — who'd been silent throughout most of the exchange — shook his head, as did Fiona. With a heavy sigh Three-D refolded the sketch and was just slipping it back into his pocket when Blaylock said, 'Wait a second. Let me see that again. I've seen it somewhere else. Leastways, the moon and star part.'

Three-D gave him the sheet and they waited silently while Blaylock studied it carefully. 'Damn,' he said suddenly. 'Of course! Catlin Construction. It's the company logo. It's on all their vehicles and paperwork!'

'You sure?'

'Absolutely. I was over there yesterday.'

'Over where?'

'The old Sunrise Motel. They bought it and the adjoining property weeks ago. They're tearing the building down even as we speak.'

'Why?'

'To build a new headquarters,' said Blaylock, adding darkly, 'At least that's what they *told* us.'

Ed and Three-D swapped thoughtful glances. Three-D said, 'Maybe we ought to check this out.'

Ed was already scooping up his hat and heading for the door. 'I'm way ahead of you, man.'

★ ★ ★

They piled into Blaylock's Suburban and drove back to town. When they reached the construction site, the Mayor parked beneath some shade trees a little farther along the street and killed the engine.

It was just after two, and the site was still very much a hive of activity. Construction workers seemed to be everywhere, engaged in one job or another, and dozers were lifting and pouring tons of dusty rubble into dumper trucks, ready for removal.

'There, see,' pointed the Mayor.

Every vehicle in sight bore the same Catlin Construction logo.

Three-D said: 'Same crescent moon and star. But no sun or second moon.'

'Is that significant?'

'I don't know.'

'So what do we do now?' asked Fiona.

'We wait,' said Ed. 'The use of that image is more than just a coincidence.'

The afternoon dragged by. Inside the SUV it grew hot and uncomfortable. Shortly after four, realising just how

210

hungry they all were, Fiona made a quick trip to *Wanda's* and bought sandwiches and coffee.

Just after six o'clock the big Van Hool motor-coach turned onto the side street and parked in the motel parking lot. With its arrival, all demolition work stopped and everyone involved switched off their engines or set down their tools and made a bee-line for it. An additional seven or eight men and women came out of the front office and also lined up to board the coach. They all wore white lab coats.

'Interesting,' murmured Ed. 'Scientists?'

'Or doctors?' said Fiona.

'Scientists or doctors,' said Three-D, 'what're they doing here? No offence, Mayor, but Dead End isn't exactly the garden spot of conventions.'

Pete Johnson waited until everyone was aboard then spoke briefly to the coach driver. As he stepped back, the coach slowly reversed onto the side street, then made a right and headed back towards Main.

'What now?' asked Blaylock.

'Follow it,' said Ed.

Blaylock started the Suburban's engine, made a U-turn and eased into traffic.

The motor-coach went as far as the high school. It then turned off the main thoroughfare and into the school parking area, where it came to a halt beside two silver Chevy Tahoes. Leaning forward over the wheel, Blaylock said quietly, 'Why the hell are they — ?'

When he fell silent, Three-D gave him a sharp glance. 'What is it, Mayor?'

Blaylock found a space across from the school playing field and parked. The sun was already sliding west, the blue sky powdering slowly to a duskier hue. 'Remember that rock band, the *Platinum Dead?*' he said.

'What about them?'

'The lead singer rented the gym so the band would have somewhere to practice. Paid cash. I charged him a stiff price for it, too, but he didn't even blink.'

'Oh-my-God,' whispered Fiona.

Everyone looked at her. To her father she said urgently: 'Remember what Wanda said just before she died?'

Blaylock stiffened. 'Wanda's *dead?*'

'What did she say?' prodded Three-D.

'After the dance. She was with Jake. She said his blood wasn't . . . human.'

★ ★ ★

For the next half hour Ed and his companions continued to watch the school, waiting for something else to happen. A little after six-thirty, the silver Catlin Construction pickup arrived with Pete Johnson behind the wheel. It turned in through the gates and parked beside the motor-coach and the two Tahoes. Johnson climbed out and so did his passengers — Jake, Beau, Brad and Kyle.

All four were wearing the same outfit — a tight-fitting black jumpsuit upon the chest of which was the now-familiar crescent-moon-and-star insignia.

'Do you think they're going to perform?' Blaylock said.

'I doubt it. They haven't brought any instruments.'

Together, the five newcomers headed for the gym.

Ed looked at the structure. It stood

apart from the rest of the school, on the far side of the playing field, a long, high-sided red-brick building with a curved glass roof.

'What the hell's going on here?' said Blaylock. 'How can we find out?'

Max finally broke his moody silence. 'Leave it to me,' he said.

★ ★ ★

The temperature inside the gym was touching a hundred-seventy-five. Six high-temperature industrial fan heaters spaced around the fringes of the echo-filled hall made sure of that. And yet the construction workers and lab technicians seated on the tiered purple benches, as well as the curious mixture of business-men, policemen and high-ranking Army officers also facing the dais that stood in the middle of the floor, were as cool as ice cubes.

Roy Drake stood on a dais before the thirty-strong group. The matt green boxes of weapons that had been delivered the previous night were stacked behind him.

A low, expectant babble rose from the crowd. They'd waited a long time for this moment. Many of them had given up all hope of ever reaching it. But the time had come at last, a time of celebration and joy for them, of death and destruction for others.

They were in fine humour.

The gymnasium doors suddenly opened and in strode Jake and his companions. But gone now was their rock star slouch: now they held themselves straight-backed and square-shouldered, chins tilted high in a gesture that was at once both proud and disdainful.

A hush settled over the assembly as they joined Drake on the dais. Jake stared out over the assembly. All eyes fixed on him. Max was watching him too, from one of the white steel joists that supported the high, curved glass roof. He hung upside-down, bat-like, from the joist, watching, waiting.

At last Jake said, 'Two thousand years ago, when our Elders first learned that our home-world was dying, they sent a group of volunteers to this planet to see if life here was possible for us. Tonight, we honour their brave souls.'

The crowd erupted with enthusiastic applause. Jake let it continue for a while, then gestured for silence.

'We must never forget how they sacrificed themselves so that our scientists could learn from them and find ways to cure, destroy or simply withstand Earth's many viruses, diseases, infections and pollutants.'

'As descendents of those volunteers, we have not only survived our stay here, but by infiltrating governments and think-tanks around the world, we've encouraged earth's scientists and entrepreneurs to design products and weapons that have actually *hastened* global warming! Within a few hundred years, the frozen hemispheres will become temperate zones, giving our people even more room to live!'

Again applause filled the room, and this time it was punctuated by enthusiastic yells and whistles.

'This is a great day, my friends. We have lived too long in secret, have for too long shaped and influenced world events from the shadows, have for too long had to *share* this planet with the enemy! But once we erect the star tower, we can guide our warships here and finally begin the total annihilation of the human race.'

As the audience went wild again, Max's jaw tightened. It was, he realised, just as Ed Knight had said: the annihilation of all that was human must inevitably lead to the annihilation of all that was *in*human.

That was something he could not let happen.

Deciding he'd heard enough, he began to inch back toward the skylight through which he'd gained entrance to the building.

'Everyone will sleep here tonight,' Jake continued. 'And then tomorrow, when construction begins — '

He broke off, head cocking to one side as his acute alien hearing picked out the smallest, softest scrape of sound above them.

His uncanny gaze saw Max as he was just beginning to squeeze back through the skylight.

'Intruder!' he screamed.

As all eyes turned to the roof, Jake

broke open one of the crates and took out an M16. Slamming a curved STANAG magazine into the weapon, he lifted it to his shoulder and fired a short burst of 5.56mm rounds that shattered the skylight but apparently missed Max.

Shards of glass fell like pellets of ice, forcing the assembled aliens to scatter. Over their alarmed cries Jake yelled: 'Kill him! He mustn't get away!'

Following his lead, Pete Johnson and the rest of the *Platinum Dead* snatched up assault rifles and fired. But their aim proved no better than Jake's, and Max vanished into the growing darkness beyond the ruined skylight.

Outside, he threw himself off the roof, landing lightly on his feet, and ran across the playing field. Seconds later, armed aliens swarmed out of the gym, quickly spotted him and began chasing him.

Jinking and weaving to make himself a difficult target, Max sprinted toward the chain-link fence. The sun had almost vanished now, and with the coming of night so too came a surge of additional strength. Another flurry of gunfire echoed across the field: bullets whined around him. Ignoring them, he vaulted the chain-link fence, momentarily staggering as he landed, and then raced for the Suburban.

Already alerted by the gunfire, Blaylock had started the engine and was waiting for Max to reach the SUV before driving away. But when Max staggered again and then clutched himself, Ed knew that the worst had happened.

'Dammit, he's been hit!'

'Father!'

Max was going so fast that he more or less slammed into the side of the SUV before he could stop himself. He ripped the rear passenger door open, flung himself inside.

Three-D yelled: '*Go, go, go!*'

By now Jake and the other aliens had made it to the fence. Cursing, Blaylock put his foot to the floor and the Chevy pulled away from the kerb with a squeal of smoking rubber.

Bullets chased them along the other-wise-quiet side street. One or two hit the tail-lights and stitched the rear bumper, and the Suburban fishtailed wildly until Blaylock fought it back under control.

'How is he?' he asked, not daring to take his eyes off the road ahead. 'Fiona? You want me to stop?'

'No. Drive to my house. He'll be all right.'

Even as she spoke, Max was pushing himself up into a more comfortable sitting position, head back, breathing deeply. As they turned out onto Main, the passing street-lamps striped him with bars of light and shadow. And as Three-D watched from the front passenger seat, the hotelier's wounds slowly began to heal.

'*Oy gevalt!*' he muttered. 'Is he an alien, too?'

'No,' said Ed. He was about to say more when Fiona flashed him a warning look. 'But he does have certain . . . uhm . . . healing powers,' he finished lamely.

'Amen to that,' Three-D said.

Before he could say more, Blaylock glanced into the rearview mirror and said, 'Shit! We got company!'

11

Ed looked over his shoulder. The Catlin Construction pickup had just turned onto Main and was coming up on them fast, headlights blazing. Ed recognised Pete Johnson behind the wheel, Jake Simms in the passenger seat.

'Can we out-run 'em, Mayor?'

'We can *try*,' said Blaylock.

He floored the accelerator and the Suburban surged forward at high-speed. Fortunately the early-evening traffic was light and there was nothing ahead to slow or stop them.

But there was nothing to slow or stop Pete Johnson either, and he immediately increased his own speed to close the gap again. The Suburban swerved wildly. The needle was bumping ninety. Blaylock found it increasingly difficult to hold the vehicle steady.

Without warning the rear window suddenly shattered and Fiona screamed.

Ed yelled for everyone to duck. Looking behind him he saw Jake pulling his head — and his M16 — back into the pickup's cab.

'Faster,' he yelled at Blaylock. 'Put your goddamn foot through the floor!'

The Mayor did his best but he couldn't widen the gap between them and the pursuing pickup.

But that wasn't the worst of it.

Even as he watched, Johnson gave the pickup more gas and it roared closer until was right on their tail, its headlights glaring in their faces.

When he was near enough, Johnson gave the gas another nudge and the pickup rammed into the rear of the SUV. The Mayor fought the wheel as the SUV lurched sideways and threatened to roll over.

While he was still struggling with it, the pickup veered off to the right and then came hurtling alongside them. From her place between Ed and Max, Fiona glanced over into the pickup's cab, made eye contact with Jake and wondered how she ever could have found him attractive.

His eyes now gleamed with hatred and his face was twisted into a snarling desire to kill.

Beside him, Johnson suddenly wrenched the wheel to the left and the truck came blasting in to give the Suburban a rough shunt that heaved it into the oncoming lane. A car coming from the other direction flashed its lights and the driver honked angrily as he quickly wheeled over, narrowly missing them.

The Suburban slipped back into the right lane, Blaylock now sweating, his breathing fast and shallow. The pickup dropped back, roared up on the left, and this time Jake brought the M16 back to his shoulder and took aim. Blaylock saw his intention and stamped on the brake.

The Suburban skidded for several yards, its back end drifting from left to right, but as it slowed and Jake finally squeezed the trigger, the pickup overshot them and his bullets missed, riddling a parked Toyota instead.

Blaylock yelled shakily: 'E-Everyone okay?'

Three-D, bracing himself against the

dashboard, muttered, '*Y'hi ratzon mil-fanekha A-donai E-loheinu* . . . '

Taking that as an affirmative, Blaylock added, 'Say one for me while you're there!'

'*Meshugener!* What do you *think* I'm doing?'

The Mayor put the Suburban back into gear and again the car leapt forward, surging up to sixty in a matter of seconds. Up ahead the pickup had also braked and was now making a hasty U-turn to come back at them. Blaylock twisted the wheel left and they turned onto a side street.

The light at the intersection fifty yards ahead was just turning red, but instead of slowing down Blaylock pushed the speed even higher.

Moments later the Suburban flashed across the junction, hit a hump in the asphalt and leapt into the air. Seconds later it landed hard, banging everyone around, and again Blaylock had to fight the wheel to keep from losing control.

Ed heard the blare of a car-horn and took another look behind them. The pickup had run the light just as a blue and white Mustang hurtled across the intersection. He felt every muscle tense as he waited for the inevitable crash. But somehow the pickup veered around the honking Mustang and kept going.

But the near-miss broke Pete Johnson's concentration and from then on he had trouble keeping the fast-moving pickup under control. The truck lurched first to the left, then curved over to the right and jumped the sidewalk. It cannoned through a *USA Today* dispenser and newspapers exploded everywhere, then scraped against a storefront and bounced off, back into the road . . . and still kept coming.

Blaylock's eyes dropped anxiously to the speedometer. The needle bumped a hundred. He looked ahead to get his bearings, saw that they were coming to another crossroads and eased his foot off the gas pedal.

Ed realised he was going to take the corner but knew they were still going too fast. 'Don't risk it, Hal!'

'You think we got a choice?'

Leaving it until the last possible moment, Blaylock wrenched the wheel right and the Suburban squealed in protest. As it swung around in a tight, wild skid the right-side wheels left the ground and the vehicle yawed over to the left. Fiona screamed; Ed yelled something unintelligible; and Three-D braced himself against the door, praying in earnest. ' . . . *ve-lohei avoteinu she-tolikhenu l'shalom v'tatz' idenu l'shalom . . .* '

The Suburban slammed back down on all four tires, shaking up everyone inside. Blaylock floored the gas again and the vehicle screeched away.

'Brace yourselves!' he yelled, and yanked the wheel hard left.

Rolling his wide eyes, Three-D whispered, ' . . . *v'tadrik-henu l'shalom, v'tagi'enu limhoz . . . AW FUCK!*'

The Chevy skidded around the corner, fishtailing madly as Blaylock kept his foot down. They were powering through the residential district now, the needle flickering around eighty-five. Blaylock looked in the rear-view mirror, saw no signs of pursuit. Relieved, he slowed down and sped along a side street that curved through the outskirts, out into dark open desert beyond.

'You can stop praying now, Three-D,' Ed said. 'I think we lost 'em.' He reached forward and patted Blaylock on the shoulder. 'Nice driving, Hal.'

Blaylock was trembling, his feverish eyes fixed firmly on the desert road ahead. He drove for another mile or so and then, unable to handle the strain any longer, pulled over and parked on the shoulder. Killing the engine and lights he slumped forward and rested his forehead on the steering wheel.

They spent the next few subdued minutes collecting themselves. Finally Three-D said gently, 'Are you okay to talk now, Max?'

Max nodded.

'What did you find out?'

He told them.

Once he'd finished, Blaylock whispered, 'This is *crazy*.'

'I wish,' said Three-D.

'What are we going to do?' the Mayor said. 'We can't just walk away and leave everyone in Dead End at their mercy.'

'They don't *have* any mercy,' Max said

quietly. 'Which means we have no choice in the matter. We fight them. We have to.'

'Christ on a cross,' said Blaylock.

He spoke for them all.

★   ★   ★

It was quiet when the Mayor drew up outside Fiona's ranch-house. They checked the surrounding darkness carefully before getting out and going inside. Fiona locked the door behind them, drew all the curtains and put coffee on to boil. Exhausted, everyone found a seat and glumly tried to decide what to do next.

After a while Three-D looked over at Max and said what they were all thinking. 'What the hell kind of chance do we have against aliens advanced enough to master interplanetary travel? Hello? Anyone here familiar with the word *massacre?*'

'Shut up, Three-D,' Ed said wearily. 'You're right about one thing, though. We can't do this alone. We'll need the help of the Settlers.'

Max, having already reached the same conclusion, said: 'They'll do as I say. I've trained them well.'

Blaylock frowned. 'Back up a minute. Why would a religious group want to — ?'

He broke off as Fiona and Max exchanged uneasy looks.

'What's going on here?' he demanded. When no-one replied he said: 'Listen! Dead End may be a whistle-stop on the way to nowhere, but as its Mayor I'm responsible for the people! Now goddammit, I want a straight answer!'

Max stared at him for a long time. Finally he said softly: 'The Settlers aren't a religious group, Hal. They're vampires. And I'm their leader.'

Silence. Horrified to have had his suspicions confirmed, Blaylock touched the bites on his neck.

'Are y-you telling me you're . . . *dead?*'

'*Un*dead,' corrected Max.

Slumped on the sofa opposite them, Three-D said, 'Excuse me, but aren't you guys forgetting something? You said Jake's blood poisoned this *tsatskeh* Wanda. So how are you going to kill the aliens if you can't *bite* 'em?'

It was a good question. But before Max could reply, they all heard a sudden, ominous whooshing sound and Ed yelled: 'Down!'

As everyone hit the floor the front door blew inward with a sound like thunder. The explosion shook the house and was followed almost immediately by several staccato bursts of automatic weapons' fire that riddled the hallway. A moment later the power went out, plunging them into darkness.

Belly-down on the floor, Ed scanned the room. Swirling dust filled the air, clogging nostrils, irritating eyes. Then, hearing Fiona cough, he called, 'Are you okay?'

'Y-Yes . . . '

'Three-D? Hal? Max?'

Stunned by the surprise attack, the others crawled through the settling dust toward him.

'Now what?' said the Mayor.

'This way,' Ed said. 'Hurry!'

As they followed him to the relative safety of the kitchen, more bullets chopped through the living room window, showering the floor with glass, stitching ragged patterns across the walls, chewing splinters out of the furniture and smashing Fiona's paintings, ornaments and keepsakes.

Ed's mind raced. He had no idea how they had managed it, but somehow the aliens had tracked them down and were determined to wipe them out before they could do anything that might spoil their plans.

The question was, what could he and the others *do* about it? They didn't have any weapons, so fighting back was out of the question. As for escape . . .

He swore. The aliens probably had the place surrounded. The minute they showed themselves, they'd be cut to pieces.

But they couldn't stay here . . .

'Well, one thing's for sure,' said Three-D, shouting to be heard above the cacophony. 'They don't have any super high-tech weapons, or they wouldn't be using ours.'

Blaylock threw him a sour look. 'Somehow I don't find that reassuring.'

Ed flinched as bullets punched holes in

the couch. 'We should've gone straight to the mine,' he said. 'We might've been able to hold them off there.'

'It's not too late,' said Fiona.

He looked at her, straining to see her face through the gloom. She gestured toward the utility room door on their left, and Ed suddenly remembered the trap-door and the tunnel below it.

New hope surged through him. 'All *right!* What're we waiting for?'

★ ★ ★

Jake tore the house apart with three more rounds from the Javelin portable anti-tank grenade launcher, then ordered the rest of his alien army to hose it down one final time with their assault rifles. When he was satisfied that no-one could have survived such a concentrated attack he yelled, 'Cease fire!'

Silence settled over the desert.

Light from the full moon showed Fiona's house to be devastated. The front elevation had been reduced to little more than rubble. The roof overhang sagged dangerously, the supporting porch-posts having been reduced to matchwood. Smoke and dust swirled lazily from the debris.

Using the Command Launch Unit's thermal view, Jake scanned the property. The only heat signature he found came from the various small fires dotted throughout the place. After a while he set the Javelin aside, took up his M16 again and approached the house at a cautious walk. As the motor-coach cruised up from where it had been waiting out in the darkness, the other aliens also broke cover and went to join him.

Although they scoured the wreckage carefully for bodies, they found none.

'Keep looking,' said Jake. 'They've got to be around here somewhere.'

'Over here,' called Pete Johnson.

Jake picked a path through the dark, rubble-strewn house to reach him, grinding glass, fine china, books and picture-frames underfoot. Johnson was standing in the charred remains of what had once been a utility room. At his feet was a trap-door that had been blown open during one of the explosions.

Jake glanced down into the darkness, saw the ladder bolted to the wall. He dropped to his knees, stuck his head through the trap and looked around.

'A tunnel,' he said as he regained his feet.

'They must have escaped through there,' Pete said. 'Let's go after them.'

'We can't. All the shelling has caused the roof to cave in.' He added: 'Where do you think it leads to?'

'The mine, most likely,' said Johnson.

'Is it far from here?'

'Two or three miles, tops.'

'All right, everybody,' Jake yelled. 'Let's go!'

★   ★   ★

After the aliens had gone, a sharp-featured coyote standing on a gentle rise overlooking what was left of the house came a little closer. He was a full-grown male, standing almost two feet at the shoulder and weighing in at around forty pounds.

By any stretch he was a magnificent specimen, his coat an unbroken light tan, his underside a startling white, a small black tip to his bushy, down-turned tail.

But there was something odd about him.

His eyes were hazel, curiously intelligent.

They were the eyes of a human.

The eyes of Sam Cocheta.

After a moment the coyote that wasn't a coyote at all turned and trotted away.

★ ★ ★

There was no telling how the vampires were going to take the news.

They took it badly.

Ethan Bayne fixed Max with a steely glare and said, 'I thought you taught us to *harvest* humans, not *help* 'em.'

'Are you questioning my orders?' demanded Max.

For a moment everyone stopped preparing for battle. At Max's orders, old strap-iron chests filled with a variety of weapons — everything from Colt revolvers to repeating rifles — had been brought out and everyone had set about arming themselves, checking their guns, the condition of their ammunition, and generally preparing to raise hell.

Bayne made no reply.

'What's the matter?' Max prodded. 'Waiting for me to turn my back, Ethan?' He made an unpleasant chuffing sound. 'After all, that's how you really earned that reputation of yours, isn't it?'

Bayne flinched as the accusation struck home. For one brief moment his right hand dropped to the butt of his .36. Back in uniform with his snake whip coiled at his belt, Max watched him closely. His eyes began to glow dangerously red.

Reluctantly Bayne backed down and limped away to join the others.

'Trouble in the ranks?' asked Ed, coming over.

'Nothing I can't handle,' Max said tersely. He eyed Ed coldly. 'Don't misunderstand my intentions. When this is over, I *will* kill you.'

Fiona broke the tension between them. 'They're here,' she whispered suddenly. 'I can feel them.'

Max cocked his head, seeming to test the damp air with his every sense. 'You're right. All right, everyone — this is it. Let's move out!'

★ ★ ★

The motor-coach pulled up outside the mine entrance and the aliens gathered together to receive last-minute orders from Jake. Nesting in a nearby tree, an owl with Sam Cocheta's eyes watched them for a few moments before taking flight. He glided silently over their heads, then swooped and flew into the mine itself.

★ ★ ★

'Are you sure this is such a good idea?' asked Three-D. 'I mean, wouldn't it be better to let the aliens come to us?'

Max flicked him a glance. They were following the contours of the main tunnel back toward the mine entrance, moving softly and cautiously, with the others strung out behind them.

'Here in the tunnel we'll have them bottled up,' he said. 'They'll be trapped, with no freedom of movement, no chance to spread out or take cover. And they won't know what hit them.'

'Trouble is, *we'll* be bottled up every bit as much as they are.'

Max smiled coolly. 'You're forgetting something. Actually, two things. One, they think they have the element of surprise. They don't. And two, they believe they're only chasing four men and one girl. When we finally meet face-to-face, they're going to encounter a force considerably greater than that.'

Three-D shrugged and tightened his grip on the Winchester he'd been given. 'I'm beginning to see why they call you colonel.'

A few yards behind them, Ed turned to Fiona and said softly, 'If we have to fall back, are there any other exits we should know about?'

She shook her head. 'Just the main entrance and the tunnel to my house. What's left of it. Every other tunnel comes to a dead end.'

He pressed his hand over hers. 'I'm sorry I got you into this, Fiona.'

'I'm not.' She kept her eyes on the shadowy tunnel ahead. 'This probably sounds corny as hell, but . . . I've lived a long time without anyone to love. You've changed that for me, and now, if I have to die, at least I can die in peace.'

'You're not gonna die,' he assured her, trying to sound more confident than he felt. 'That's a promise.'

She smiled and said, 'You talk too much.'

Then she reached up and kissed him.

Marching along behind them, Hal Blaylock raised his eyebrows and shook his head.

Then:

Max suddenly stopped and raised his hand. At once everything around them went absolutely quiet, absolutely still. Taking up positions on either side of the tunnel, some kneeling, some standing, the defenders braced themselves, waiting, watching. Blaylock's mouth went dry. Three-D wiped sweat off his forehead. Ed's jaw clamped firm.

An owl came swooping out of the darkness. It flew over their heads and then was gone, headed for the cavern they'd just left. Ed wondered vaguely where in hell it had come from and what it was doing down here at this of all times.

Then Max yelled: 'Here they come!'

★ ★ ★

The weapon-heavy aliens exploded out of the tunnel ahead with Jake in the lead, screaming wildly as they charged forward, firing as they came. There was no pretence at strategy. Jake's plan was brutally simple: to overwhelm the enemy with a frontal assault and hope that numbers, surprise and persistence would carry the day.

It very nearly did.

For one brief moment the vampires were frozen by the suddenness of the assault. Then Ed shouted, 'Now!' and started firing the old Spencer carbine he'd been issued.

The vampires followed his example and the tunnel shuddered to the crack and whine of ricocheting bullets. The aliens ran straight into a wall of lead and orange blood spurted from their wounded bodies.

But the vampires suffered casualties too in those first hectic seconds, as 5.56mm rounds smacked into male and female vampires alike.

On the surface it was, as Three-D had predicted, a massacre. But even as they were hammered backwards by the onrushing aliens, the vampires began to heal. All the withering gunfire could do was slow them down or distract them, but there was no way it was ever going to kill them.

Unfortunately, it was the same with the aliens. Bullets hit them and knocked them down, but conventional weapons couldn't keep them down.

Max emptied his Winchester into them until he was out of bullets. Then it was close-quarter, hand-to-hand and no-holds-barred.

Hurling the rifle aside, he reached into his tunic pocket and brought out two small copper disks with razor-sharp edges. He scanned the oncoming aliens until he spotted Jake and then hurled them at him.

Jake dodged to one side and the first disk spun on to bury itself in the rock wall beside him. But he wasn't quick enough to avoid the second.

The disk sliced through his left wrist and the hand fell twitching to the floor. With a roar he brought his M16 up in his right hand and fired a three-round burst in Max's direction. Moving faster than the eye could follow, Max dove behind a pile of brittle cholera-victim bones.

A group of aliens charged forward to be met by three of the deserters. The aliens fired from the hip and the deserters jerked and spun as the bullets cored through their flesh. But in the next moment they started returning fire with their breech-loading trapdoor Springfields, and .45/.70 rounds punched the aliens back again, the remaining two deserters hacking and chopping at them with curved military sabres before their wounds could heal.

Jake bent to scoop up his dismembered hand. He held it against the ragged, orange-blood-soaked stump of his left forearm and gritted his teeth as the flesh began to sizzle, the hand and wrist fusing seamlessly back together.

Meanwhile, Pete Johnson aimed an M79 grenade launcher at Charlie Steel-good. The big mechanic had elected to go into battle with the tool of his former trade — his blacksmith's heavy club hammer, and he'd just smashed Roy Drake to the ground when Johnson got him lined up and took up first pressure on the two-stage trigger of the stubby, high-stock launcher.

Before he could make the shot, a .56-calibre slug whacked him in the face and tore off the back of his skull as it exited. Johnson staggered back and collapsed.

Steelgood spun around and waved his thanks to Ed.

Ed grinned, snatched up the launcher and tore the bag of grenades off Johnson's shoulder.

Several yards further along the tunnel, Max had confronted a bunch of charging aliens with the full intensity of his flame-red eyes. The two leading aliens immediately corkscrewed to the ground, seemingly fried by the power he wielded. The rest hit him with a lengthy burst of automatic weapons' fire and he staggered under its impact — but was healing again even as he fell back to his own lines.

Three-D kept firing into the alien horde, emptying first his long gun, then tearing a handgun from his waistband. It was fire, thumb back and fire again, all the while hoping that a miracle would happen and they could actually drive the aliens back.

Then Hal Blaylock cried out and spilled backwards.

As he hit the ground, Ed and Three-D ran to his aid and set about trying to check the flow of blood coming from the wound in his left shoulder.

Three-D spotted Fiona and gestured urgently. 'The Mayor's been hit!'

Face flushed by the heat of battle, she crawled over and briefly examined the wound. Breathing hard, his sweat-run face as pale as paper, Blaylock asked her how bad it was.

'The bullet passed right through,' she said. 'Once we stop the bleeding you'll be fine.'

As she spoke, she tore off one of her shirt-sleeves and used it to bind his shoulder. Ed felt a heady rush of admiration as he watched her and saw just how cool she was under fire.

'My gun, give me my gun,' Blaylock said as soon as she was finished.

Fiona handed it to him. 'Try not to move around too much, Hal.'

Rising, she spotted an alien about to leap at them over a pile of rocks and fixed him with eyes that suddenly spat white-hot flame. The alien was flung backwards, two smoking holes burned right through his heart.

'What the hell do you need guns for, if you can do that?' Ed said.

'Because I can't do it more than a few times in succession,' she said. 'None of us can, not even my father. It saps too much strength.'

Grabbing her gun, she and Ed went back to emptying their weapons into the oncoming aliens.

By now, however, it had become clear that this was one battle they couldn't hope to win. The aliens had them outnumbered and outgunned. That said, the best the vampires could do now was organise some kind of fighting retreat.

'Fall back!' Max shouted. 'Fall back to the cavern!'

As the vampires and their human allies did just that, dragging their wounded and wounded-but-healing comrades with them, Max stabbed a finger at Bayne and yelled, 'Cover us!'

Bayne grinned, his dark eyes suddenly flaring to life. This was more like it. Going out to meet the challengers, just like the old days . . .

He broke cover and strode forward to meet the oncoming aliens with both Navy Colts blazing, setting up such a torrent of fire that the aliens were bowled backwards before him.

Ed, Fiona and Three-D also stood their ground, adding their own firepower to Bayne's. But it was useless, and soon they too had to fall back and join the others as they hurried back toward the cavern.

The first ones to enter the chamber immediately sought fresh cover and began reloading their weapons. As Ed and his companions jogged through the entrance and headed for the back of the cave, he was struck by the futility of trying to fight a war against people — things — who couldn't die.

'We've got to get out of here,' he said as they rejoined Max. 'We need to buy time, come up with a new plan of attack, find some way of keeping those bastards down for good.'

'And how do you propose to do that?'

'Are you sure these other tunnels are all blocked off?'

'Yes.'

'Damn!'

'One can save you.'

They turned, startled not only by the unexpectedly calm voice but also by finding Sam Cocheta standing behind them, calmly tucking the owl feather back into his snakeskin hatband.

'Where the hell did you spring from?' asked Ed.

'Not important,' Sam said. 'Here to pay

debt. *That* important.'

Three-D said, 'I've sensed you around me a lot just lately, *zaken*.'

'It is good for friends to watch out for each other.'

'Amen,' said Three-D.

Suddenly Bayne came chasing back into the cavern. Moments later the aliens made an attempt to storm the cavern entrance. A wall of lead held them back, at least temporarily.

'Anasazi, in Navaho,' Sam continued, 'means 'enemy from afar.''

'For crissake, Chief,' Ed said, 'we don't have time for any hokey Indian shit!'

'What're you getting at, Old One?' Three-D said to Sam.

'In the distant past the Anasazi once lived in peace with the aliens. Then one day they found out that the aliens planned to destroy mankind and attacked them. But the aliens were too strong. They killed most of the Anasazi and drove the rest away.'

'You saying it's the aliens the Navajo were referring to?' asked Ed.

''Enemy from afar,'' said Three-D. 'It

fits.' He looked at Sam again. 'What's your point?'

'Tonight I help you destroy the murderers of my ancestors.'

Ed threw another anxious look toward the cavern entrance. The aliens were slowly but surely gaining ground. The defending vampires were steadily being forced back. Making a snap decision, Ed pointed to the left-side tunnel and said, 'Take that one. I'll buy you some time.'

'No, Ed!' Fiona grabbed his arm. 'You can't!'

Ed looked at her, hating the horror he saw in her expression, the certainty that she would never see him again. Then he pulled his arm free and told Three-D: 'Take her with you, partner.'

Three-D grabbed Fiona by the arm, but she easily broke away and stood her ground. 'If we're going to die,' she said. 'We'll die together.'

Ed stared at her, a lump growing in his throat. There was suddenly so much he wanted to say to her, things he would never now get the chance to say.

Just then Max stepped between them.

Grave-faced, he said, 'Go — both of you! *I'll* stay.'

Ed's shook his head. 'We'll both stay.'

'No! You and Fiona have too much to live for. I see that now.' He turned to his daughter and said gently: 'Fiona. For your mother's sake.'

Tears ran down Fiona's smudged cheeks. Her mouth worked, but nothing came out. At last she managed one choking sentence.

'Remember, father — if you bite one, you'll die.'

'Go!' he ordered.

Fiona kissed him on the cheek. Then Ed grasped her arm and dragged her away from Max, into the left-hand tunnel.

Sam, Three-D, Blaylock and the other vampires hurried after them.

12

When they were gone, Max turned his attention to the oncoming aliens. For the first time in too long he felt completely free. There was no longer any need to hide his true nature behind the genial façade of a hotel proprietor. Now, at last, he was free to be exactly what he was: a *vampire*. A *leader* of vampires.

He transformed quickly, allowing all that was Undead to come raging to the surface. Ridges of bone stood proud along his brow. His eyes sank back into his head and burned with a fierce crimson brilliance. His cheekbones thrust forward, hollowing out the cheeks themselves, and when he opened his mouth in a snarl, baring his fangs, his snarl was so loud and primeval that the oncoming aliens actually broke step and faltered briefly.

Recognising the challenge in the sound, Jake pushed forward to confront Max, his black eyes wide, sparking anger and hatred for this enemy whose measure he still couldn't quite get.

'Step aside,' he said.

Max's head sank into his raised shoulders and his hands twisted into claws. 'Not a chance.'

With a snarl that was pure beast, Jake flung his M16 aside and threw himself at Max. They came together with a harsh slam of flesh against flesh, each grabbing the other in a hold that was designed to throw his opponent off his feet.

Jake pushed Max back two yards, then Max retaliated in kind and it was all Jake could do to hold his ground.

A moment later Jake shifted his weight and Max lost his balance. Jake immediately seized the advantage and swung him around. He released his grip and Max flew sideways and crashed into the cavern wall with enough force to shatter rock.

He fell to the ground but came back up almost at once and charged Jake. They collided again and Jake was thrown backwards. Before he could recover Max was on him, firing rapid, powerful punches, left, right, left, right, the blows coming so fast they appeared as a blur to those watching.

Orange blood squirted from Jake's nose and ran from the corner of his belligerent mouth. But incredibly when he showed his teeth it was not in a grimace, but a grin.

He blocked Max's next crushing blow, threw one of his own that mashed Max's nose with a sharp cracking of cartilage, then grabbed him by his ears and hurled him away.

Max slammed into the cavern wall, the force cracking the jagged rock, and slumped to the ground. Jake dragged him up again and savagely began to beat his head, face-first, against the wall.

Around them, the other aliens watched in approval, blood-lust making their eyes shine.

Max made a feeble attempt to break free but it was useless. Face battered and bleeding, he started to lose consciousness and Jake felt a savage flare of victory rush through him.

But Max wasn't finished yet.

Summoning all his strength, he sank to

his haunches so that he could twist around and then power back up, grabbing Jake by his shoulders, lifting him overhead and then throwing him into the alien onlookers.

Jake crashed into his companions, sending several of them sprawling. Not waiting for him to recover, Max grasped him by the neck and flung him against the wall. Dazed, Jake sank to the ground. Max was on him instantly. He rained blows at Jake's face, finishing with an uppercut that snapped his head back. Max then grabbed him by the throat and started to strangle him . . .

His thumbs and fingers pushed ever deeper into the flesh of Jake's throat. Max leaned close and stared into Jake's contorted face. His blazing red eyes locked onto Jake's cold black eyes.

Jake opened his mouth as if to say something. Instead, he stiffened as Max's fingers finally punctured the skin and dug into the meat of Jake's neck, chewing up the flesh as they pushed inexorably deeper still . . .

Orange blood spilled from Jake's

mouth and his eyes widened until they almost spilled from their sockets. Now it was Max who felt victory was within his grasp, and he smiled a demonic smile that bared his long, silver-coloured fangs.

'Die!' he hissed.

His triumph was short-lived.

Jake suddenly thrust up with both arms, breaking Max's stranglehold, and butted him in the face with his forehead. Stunned, Max staggered back.

Around them the aliens went wild.

Jake grabbed Max by throat and crotch and lifted him effortlessly overhead. He then dropped to his haunches and brought Max down across his upraised knee. Max's spine snapped and he dangled limply in his opponent's grasp.

Jake threw him to the ground. Quickly straddling him, Jake pinned him with his knees, grasped his head with both hands and wrenched, breaking Max's neck.

He then rose and turned to the other aliens.

'Death to our enemies!'

The aliens roared their approval.

Jake went to one of the old timbers

supporting the roof, tore off a long splinter the size of a spike and returned beside Max.

Helpless, Max watched as Jake raised the wooden spike and then plunged it into the vampire's heart.

Max screamed. His eyes turned brilliantly red and his body glowed white — and then a searing flame engulfed his body and within seconds he was dead. The flame vanished as quickly as it came and when it was gone, so was Max.

Not even a trace of his ashes remained.

And there was no-one left to hold the aliens back any longer.

★ ★ ★

Ed and Sam led the way along the tunnel, with Fiona, Three-D, Blaylock and the surviving vampires following closely on their heels. The tunnel was unlit, but the walls were streaked with peculiar white veins which gave off a fluorescent glow.

Three-D pointed to them as they ran. 'These rocks are like those white pebbles,' he reminded Ed.

'Miners dug these tunnels,' Sam said, 'and dumped the waste in the desert.'

'So that's why you find them on the ground,' said Three-D. '*Ech*, it's freezing down here!'

'Underground glaciers flowed through here back in the Ice Age,' said Ed. Immediately he frowned and said, 'How the hell did I know that?'

Sam's only response was a faint, knowing smile.

They ran on.

After another hundred yards or so, Hal Blaylock stopped and leaned against one of the glowing walls. 'Go on without me,' he gasped, his breath fogging in the cold air. 'I'm only . . . slowing you . . . down.'

'You can make it,' Ed assured him. 'It's not much farther.'

'What isn't?' asked Three-D.

Ed frowned. 'Good question.' He looked at Sam. 'What's going on, Chief? Feels like something's feeding me information. Or maybe some*one*?'

Again Sam only smiled.

Realizing he wasn't going to get anything out the stoic Apache, Ed slipped his arm around the Mayor and helped him to stagger on. The others followed.

Ahead, the tunnel split in two. Ed pulled up and signalled for everyone to stop. The tunnel on their left had partly caved-in at some time in the distant past. A huge pile of rocks blocked off most of the entrance, but there was still a small, dark hole visible near the top.

Ed said: 'All of you, start climbing till you reach the other side.'

'Why?' asked Three-D.

'Just *do* it, *chaver!*'

'But we can't hold them off up there.'

Sam put a rough hand on Three-D's shoulder. 'Not hold. Hide. Hurry.'

Ed said: 'Trust me, Three-D. I know what I'm doing. I don't know why, but I do.'

'Well, I'm glad one of us does.' Three-D took Fiona's hand and helped her climb up the rocks. The Mayor wearily followed them.

'We must go,' Sam told Ed.

Ed nodded. But he stood there a few more moments watching as Fiona neared the top of the rock-fall.

Finally, she reached the hole. She paused before she ducked into the dark shaft beyond and looked back at Ed. 'Now what?' she asked.

'Keep quiet,' he said. 'Don't make a sound or they'll hear you.'

Motioning for Sam to follow, he led the Apache into the other tunnel.

As they disappeared into the darkness there came sounds of pursuit.

* * *

Almost forgetting to breathe, Three-D watched the glowing tunnel from a peephole between two fallen rocks. As he listened to the sounds of the aliens drawing closer, he felt Fiona huddle beside him. He put his arm around her, hoping to comfort her.

'What was that prayer you were saying back in Hal's car?' she whispered.

'I was asking God to deliver us from danger.'

'Might be a good idea to say it again.'

Three-D nodded and they fell silent.

Beside them the Mayor crossed himself

and said a quiet prayer of his own.

The noise of the approaching aliens grew louder. Three-D squinted through the peephole and suddenly caught the first flash of movement in the glowing darkness beyond the rock-fall. His tension seemed to communicate itself to the others, and he felt their apprehension fill the cramped dead-end tunnel. It made him feel even more like a rat trapped in a barrel.

Jake came into sight first, followed closely by the others. His black jumpsuit was mottled by orange and red stains. But Jake himself appeared to be uninjured, which could only mean one thing — Max was no more.

Fiona, peering through another peephole, realised it too, and she closed her eyes in despair.

Jake moved slowly, his breath misting before his face. Three-D noticed that none of the aliens looked as fresh as they had at the start of this nightmare. *Well,* he thought grimly, *if nothing else, we've at least given these mamzers a run for their money.*

Below, Jake stopped and looked at the blocked tunnel to his left.

Three-D told himself it was just his imagination, but it seemed as if Jake was staring right through the rocks at him.

Jake tilted his head back a little. He seemed to be testing the cold subterranean air.

Three-D tightened his grip on his Winchester. Behind him the remaining vampires stirred uneasily. Blaylock's pained breathing suddenly sounded unnaturally loud.

In the tunnel, the aliens began to shift restlessly, eager to continue the chase.

But Jake wasn't about to be rushed. He continued to stare at the rock-fall and finally took a step toward it.

Sweat ran down Three-D's forehead, dripped off his left eyebrow.

He knows we're here. He can sense us.

A sound deep inside the right-hand tunnel caught Jake's attention. He stopped and looked into the darkness. Then with a gloating smile, he signalled for the others to follow him.

They filed slowly past the rock-fall,

looking worn down by the cold but still deadly dangerous.

* * *

As they jogged along the right-hand tunnel, their breath clouding the frigid air, Ed glanced at the old Apache and said: 'Since we may not get out of this alive, there's something I'd like to know.'

Sam spoke without turning his head. 'Why I was expecting you when you broke down in the desert?'

'So you're a mind-reader as well as a shape-shifter, are you?'

'Like you, there are things about me that I must accept without question.'

The words jolted Ed to a stop. 'You know about *that*, too?' he said quietly.

'It is not just a white man's curse,' said Sam. 'There were people like you among my ancestors.'

'Well, that's a comfort.'

They hurried on.

'Are you sure this is going to work?' Ed said.

'You are full of questions.'

'Only when my ass is on the line.'

'Yes, it will work — if the gods are watching over us.'

'That's not much of a guarantee.'

'Some things must be taken on trust.'

'Such as a half-assed plan and a hokey Indian spell?'

Sam shot him a sour look. 'They will not see us until it is too late. Of that I am sure. I have used the Invocation before, many times. It has never failed me yet.'

'Always a first t — '

Sam cut him off. 'You talk too much.'

A hundred yards on Sam slowed to a more cautious pace. Without warning, the tunnel ended in a deep black shaft. He picked up a pebble and dropped it into the pit. It took forever to hit the bottom. Ed looked up to see some sort of narrow funnel leading to the surface. Far, far above, he could just make out the full moon: then clouds drifted in and hid it from view.

Hearing the aliens coming, they quickly retraced their steps until they came to a gentle curve in the tunnel which had been shored-up with ancient timbers. Splitting up, they each hid behind a timber, opposite one another.

Sam made a series of quick movements with his gnarled hands as he muttered, '*Uranun caripe beglen ol gemeganza denoan chiis gosaa zamicmage oleo lag-sapah arphe oresa ethamz taa tabegisoroch zodinu ar zurah paremu zodimibe papnorge maninua zonac dodsih hoxmarch train amonons pare sad niis kures.*'

When he was finished, Ed waited expectantly for something to happen. It didn't. He looked at himself, at the bag of grenades over his shoulder, at the ugly-looking M79 he'd taken from Pete Johnson — nothing had changed. There was no magic tingling sensation, no out-of-body experience. He looked across at Sam and rasped, 'You know something, Chief? Your invisibility charm sucks.'

Sam held one finger to his lips for silence.

They waited.

A few seconds later Jake led his troops into view. They were still moving slowly, but apparently more from exhaustion than any sense of caution. Jake stopped, stared into the darkness ahead. Ed, hardly daring to breath, wondered if he'd seen them, or whether he could just sense that something up ahead wasn't quite right.

Then, at last, Jake continued forward.

It seemed to take him forever to draw level with the pit-props, but it was actually only seconds. Once there he stopped again, no more than two feet from where Ed was desperately trying to shrink back into the darkness.

Jake looked from left to right. Then directly at where Ed was hiding.

Ed froze, thinking: *That's it. We're done for* . . .

But then, incredibly, Jake moved on again and Ed felt almost light-headed. Jake really *hadn't* seen him. Sam's hokey Indian magic had worked after all!

But they weren't out of the woods yet.

Jake wearily kept going. The other aliens followed him, equally exhausted but thinking only of the slaughter to come when they finally ran their enemies to ground.

One after another they shuffled by . . . just over thirty in all, including Beau,

Brad, Kyle, Pete Johnson, Roy Drake, the sharp-suited businessmen, the policemen, Army officers, Catlin construction workers and lab technicians . . .

When the last one had stumbled past, Ed cat-footed out of his niche and raised the M79. Somewhere in the darkness ahead Jake came to the edge of the pit and shouted: 'Wait!'

Ed thought: *The hell with that.*

He pulled the trigger. The weapon made a low, distinctive thump of sound as it fired a 40 × 46mm high-explosive grenade down the tunnel after the aliens.

Ed threw himself back against the wall, already breaking open the weapon and fumbling a second grenade from the bag into the breech. He waited for the explosion. None came. His heart sank. He wondered whether the grenade had been a dud.

In fact, the grenade was designed not to arm itself until it had travelled a distance of ninety feet.

Then —

It went off with a gigantic smack of sound, the force of it rushing upwards and outwards to hammer at the mine's walls and roof and smash into the unsuspecting aliens and shove them toward the shaft at the tunnel's end.

Ignoring the hot back-blast of air, Ed stepped out again, braced the M79 against his hip and fired the second grenade. Again there came that dull whump; again a fraction of a second passed before the second explosion rocked the tunnel and cuffed and pummelled the aliens ever closer to the lip of the shaft.

By now the aliens were screaming in fear, surprise and rage, but the explosions had rendered Ed deaf to everything save a high-pitched whine to which he paid no mind.

He reloaded, fired off a third HE grenade, and beyond the wall of dust and falling debris, the aliens at the front of the group finally lost their footing and starting spilling over the edge and into the darkness below.

Ed launched another grenade, and now he could hardly breathe for the billowing dust and displaced dirt sifting from the tunnel roof. Doggedly he went forward into the haze, reloaded and sent his penultimate grenade down the tunnel. There was a flash of blinding white light and another ear-punishing explosion that almost knocked him over. But pay-back felt so good right then that he hardly even felt it.

At last the roar and rumble began to die down and he turned and looked back at Sam, whose lined face was as dust-darkened as his own.

Sam's only response was a brief smile. It had worked, just as he'd said it would. Thrown down into the depths of the earth where they could never hope to survive the sub-zero cold, the only thing the aliens could look forward to now was a slow, agonising death.

Ed stumbled back toward him, holding the M79 down by his side. He put one arm around the Apache's shoulders and said, 'I'm sorry I doubted you, Chief.'

Sam shrugged. 'Buy me a drink and we'll call it even.'

They walked a few yards back along the tunnel. Now there was only one thing left to do: send the final grenade into the roof and seal this subterranean passage off forever.

But even as he started loading the M79 for the final time, Ed thought he heard a sound.

A sound coming from beyond the slowly-settling dust.

A chill tingled his spine. He looked at Sam. Sam nodded. He'd heard it too.

Someone in there was still alive.

Alive and coming back for them.

Suddenly Jake burst out of the dust-cloud. Hatred contorted his mangled face. He came at great speed and grabbed Ed before he could move. He grasped Ed around the throat, picked him up and began strangling him, savage grunts escaping from deep inside him.

Ed kicked his feet but couldn't break the hold. Sam hurled himself onto Jake's back, but Jake let go with one hand and swatted Sam aside as if he were no more than a fly.

Sam hit the tunnel floor and rolled.

Jake turned back to Ed, rammed him up against the tunnel wall and started pounding the life out of him. Powerless to stop him, Ed felt the pain of the alien's blows ripping through him. Dazed and bleeding, he fought not to black out.

Then, all at once, Jake stopped and held him at arm's-length. 'Before I finish you,' he said venomously, 'I want you to see what you've done!'

He dragged Ed by the hair into the swirling dust and over piles of fallen rock until they reached the edge of the shaft. There he thrust Ed to his hands and knees, said, 'Look!'

Bleary-eyed, Ed glanced down into the shaft. By the light of the full moon still visible through the funnel above, he saw the remains of the aliens sprawled in a chaotic heap at the bottom of the pit. It was so cold down there that they were already dusted white with ice.

'Does it give you a good feeling?' demanded Jake. 'Does it make you feel proud to commit genocide?'

He picked Ed up and hurled him against the wall. Ed fell into a huddle, his body throbbing with agonizing pain.

But something else was also coursing

through his body. It slowly replaced the pain and began filling him with new energy, bulking him out and changing his appearance.

The full moon . . .

It's happening again, he thought. *It's happening again* . . .

Jake stood spread-legged before Ed, towering over him, allowing his own fury to combat the numbing chill to which his race had never been able to adapt. His eyes were wide, wild, his lips drawn back in a mad grin of satisfaction: at least he would take with him the destroyer of his people.

Then Ed looked up at him, and Jake's grin faded.

For now he was confronted not by Ed the human, but Ed the animal.

The wolf.

The *werewolf*.

Ed rose up wide and tall, at once immensely powerful and yet lean and graceful. His face was essentially Ed's face, but the characteristics had changed. The nose and lower jaw had elongated to form a wolf's snout and rough, spiky hair covered his skin. The tips of his ears had sharpened to points and his eyes, too, had become a cool, predatory yellow.

He stood on his hind legs and gave a howl that echoed throughout the tunnel. As he did so his jaws opened to show razor-sharp fangs.

Then he leapt at Jake.

He came in fast, swiping and raking and growling and Jake all but wilted before the assault. He brought his arms up to protect himself. But Ed drove him back with one gouging blow after another, and soon Jake was bleeding orange fluid from a dozen deep, ragged wounds.

He desperately swung a punch, catching Ed on the jaw. But that only fuelled Ed's fury. He slammed Jake to the ground and they rolled over and over, wrestling for control, each trying to destroy the other.

Werewolf and alien, they rolled ever closer to the edge of the pit.

Jake clamped Ed's jaws shut, fixed his other hand around Ed's shaggy throat and tried to throttle him. Ed twisted loose and clamped his fangs on Jake's face. Jake screamed as a chunk of flesh was torn from his cheek, and fell back.

Ed was on him instantly. His fingertips were now claws and he dug them into Jake, wrenched him up off the ground and howled long and loud at the moon above.

Jake cried out in fear.

Ed ignored him.

As his howl ended he threw Jake into the pit, there to spend an eternity frozen in ice.

★　★　★

Three-D and the others listened to the silence for a long moment. After the sounds of combat, and then the chilling series of howls and snarls, followed by the crash and crunch of a prolonged cave-in, the stillness and silence had an ominous quality to it.

At last, able to stand the suspense no more, he clambered out from behind the rocks and peered below into the tunnel on his right.

The last of the dust was still floating lazily around him.

Fiona broke cover next, then Blaylock and Dolan, Bayne, Steelgood and the other vampires. Everyone seemed subdued by the events of the long night.

Three-D looked at Fiona. The concern was clear to see in her face. Had they won or lost? Was Ed alive or —

He was about to say something — he didn't really know what, most likely some meaningless phrase that was meant to offer comfort — when he caught a movement from the corner of his eye and turned back to the wall of dust.

He waited.

They all waited.

And then . . .

Ed, bruised and bleeding but back in human form, stumbled towards them, his left arm draped around Sam's sloping shoulders.

Fiona scrambled down the rocks and ran to Ed, who hugged her with his free arm.

The others quickly descended to the ground. For a while no-one spoke. It was enough just to know that they'd beaten the enemy and ensured their own survival. Then Ed started walking slowly again, still holding onto Fiona and Sam, and the others fell into step behind them.

'How did you know they couldn't survive the cold?' Fiona asked after a while.

Ed nodded toward Sam. 'Ask him.'

Fiona looked at the Apache, who said only, 'Mind Whispering.'

'Mind Whispering?'

'Apache for telepathy,' guessed Three-D.

'Spiritfolk speak to his mind,' Sam said.

Ed shrugged. 'News to me.'

'And just who are these 'Spiritfolk'?' asked Three-D.

'My ancestors,' said Sam. 'When the aliens defeated the Anasazi and took over their cliff dwellings, Star Woman came down from the sky and made the winter so severe that it drove the aliens out. They have been prisoners of the cold ever since.'

Ed watched Three-D carefully. He could just imagine his companion's reaction to that; he was a man of science and that kind of stuff was pure Pueblo Indian fantasy.

But to his surprise, Three-D said: 'It works for me.'

At length they emerged from the mine into the pale silvery light of pre-dawn.

Charlie Steelgood turned to Ed. 'Knight?'

'Uh-huh?'

'What happens now?'

Ed stopped and faced him. Without being aware of it, they had broken into two groups, vampires on one side, Ed, Fiona, Three-D, Blaylock and Sam on the other.

'The truce ends at noon,' he said quietly.

'You'll be coming after us?' said Bayne.

Ed fixed him with a steady look. 'With every wooden stake I can find.' He looked at his companions. 'Let's go.'

Bayne waited until they had their backs to him, then drew his Colt and aimed at Ed's broad shoulders.

'Why wait till noon?' he said.

Ed and the others froze.

Bayne grinned and was about to put a

bullet in Ed's spine . . . when the cold barrel of another gun pressed against the nape of his neck. He stiffened, turned slowly, and found himself facing Quincy Dolan and the fancy Philadelphia Derringer that was aimed at his forehead.

'Bad idea,' said Dolan.

Bayne's crimson eyes sparked with hate. 'Got religion all of a sudden, Quince?'

He started to thumb back the Colt's hammer and shoot Dolan in the belly, but Dolan beat him to it, planting a .41 calibre Rimfire cartridge right between his eyes.

Bayne staggered back, eyes bugged with surprise. Then he slowly collapsed, his newly-acquired 'third eye' turned toward the rising sun.

Steelgood looked down at him. 'Reckon I forgot to tell you,' he said. 'I forged Dolan's bullets from the last of your silver dollars.'

Bayne had just enough time for Dolan's words to register before a sudden, short-lived burst of flame incinerated him.

Dolan turned to find Ed and the others

looking at him. He was thinking about a girl called Cathy Maynard when he said: 'We may always be vampires, Mr Knight, but that doesn't mean we always have to be the dregs of humanity.'

Looking him in the eye, Ed considered that. He considered a lot of things in those few seconds before he replied; about the difference between what a man did out of pure meanness and what he did simply to survive; about how much difference there really was between a vampire and a werewolf; and how perhaps even the undead could learn a different and maybe better way to exist.

Three-D must have been thinking along the same lines, because he said softly, 'It's the Seekers' job to track down monsters. But I don't see any monsters here, do you, *chaver?*'

'No, I don't think I do,' Ed said. 'But I *do* think we've swapped one enemy for another.'

'The aliens?' said Fiona.

'You heard what your father had to say,' he told her. 'We've won a battle today, not a war. They're still out there, no telling how many. They've infiltrated political systems, police forces, the military might across the world. But now we know how to fight them . . . how to hunt them down and destroy them.'

Dolan smiled and said: 'If we can ever help . . . ?'

'I'll remember that,' said Ed, and shook hands with him.

As the vampires made their way back into the mine, Blaylock cleared his throat. 'Can we get moving now?' he asked irritably. 'My shoulder's hurting like a bitch, and I need Fiona to patch it up properly.'

But Ed's mind was elsewhere. 'You know something, Hal?'

'What?'

'I think today might be a good day to rename the town Silverton.'

'You talk too much,' Three-D told him. 'Shut him up for me, will you, Fiona?'

'My pleasure,' she said.

And smiling, she moved close to Ed and did just that.

THE END

We do hope that you have enjoyed reading this large print book.

Did you know that all of our titles are available for purchase?

We publish a wide range of high quality large print books including:
Romances, Mysteries, Classics
General Fiction
Non Fiction and Westerns

Special interest titles available in large print are:
The Little Oxford Dictionary
Music Book, Song Book
Hymn Book, Service Book

Also available from us courtesy of Oxford University Press:
Young Readers' Dictionary
(large print edition)
Young Readers' Thesaurus
(large print edition)

For further information or a free brochure, please contact us at:
Ulverscroft Large Print Books Ltd.,
The Green, Bradgate Road, Anstey,
Leicester, LE7 7FU, England.
Tel: (00 44) **0116 236 4325**
Fax: (00 44) **0116 234 0205**

THE MULTI-MAN

John Russell Fearn

Research biologist Jeffrey Dexter's experiments produce a creature capable of endless reproduction, yet lacking human reserve. Then he's murdered — swept aside by the ruthless Multi-Man. Dexter's wife's claim, that the new Jeffrey Dexter is only a cellular duplicate of her husband, finds her incarcerated in an institution for the mentally unbalanced. Dexter No 2 develops his plans: famous people are duplicated to nominate Dexter's Presidency in a new scientific era. Can Scotland Yard Detective Sergeant Hanbuy hold him back?

MAKE IT NYLONS

Gordon Landsborough

Joe P. Heggy, professional trouble-buster for an international construction firm, is travelling to Turkey. As the plane lands in Istanbul he looks out of the window and witnesses a murder — a man being stabbed. The victim was the leader of the country's Ultra-Nationalist Party. That glimpse of murder brings him trouble. Millions of fanatics try to pin the crime on him — his life is in danger. His only ally — an Amazonian Rumanian peasant with a passion for western nylons!